The H

J Edward Neill

Cover Art by Tahina Morrison

ISBN-13: 978-1523380381
ISBN-10: 1523380381

Hecatomb - ˈhekəˌtōm/ (noun) – *An extensive loss of life for some cause*

The Hecatomb is *non-sequitur*. Meaning the four stories herein are not in chronological order.

It's up to you, the reader, to determine the true order of events. It's possible different readers will decide on different orders. I say possible; what I mean is I hope it's true. I want every one of you to come away with a dissimilar, yet equally terrifying experience.

I also want you to read this alone. Preferably at night. Beneath a lamp in an otherwise dark room.

I want you to feel what I felt as I wrote it.

But I'm not telling you what the feeling was…

Contents

Old Man of Tessera

I still remember the eve I came to the city of Tessera.

I remember meeting the withered old tile maker who lived in the house nearest the sea. I remember all the things he said to me, all the things he did. I remember what it came to in the end.

I was only twenty and two in those strange, surreal days. Before the storms came, the world still had its wonder for me. I had believed in all the foolish things young men put their faith in. I had loved a girl and lost her. I had learned to ride, to fish, to sail, and to fight. I was a lad with a future. Life might have been good, if not for the way it happened.

Had the storm not waylaid my own city and slain so many of those I loved, I would never have come to Tessera. But as it happened, it did. A week after my family drowned, I set out alone. With a bag of bread and a heart heavy as stone, I rode east along the old cliffs until my pitiful steed and I shambled onto a cobbled road. It was raining that night. I was sodden with self-pity, soaked to my skinny bones with rain, but I was not quite ready to die. I saw a city, its lanterns gleaming in the black. *Home,* I hoped right away. I should have kept riding.

The old man took me in that very night. His name was Hasai. He was some five and eighty along, as skinny as a stick, as knobby and crabbed as an old piece of driftwood. His house atop the cliff was nearest the sea and first along the road to Tessera. I saw the warm lights in his windows and the rain rolling off his eaves, and I went to his door. I must have looked like a fish, all wet in my father's cloak, my eyes wide and my skin clammy as a cod. I thought he would shove me off his porch and into the angry waters off the cliff's edge, but no. He looked me over and locked his fingers around my wrist. "Come in, you sodden soul," he said to me. "I've some soup on the fire. This rain'll be the death of you, same as your village. You are from Veni, aren't you?"

He was right. I was from Veni. Though of course, Veni was no more. The storms had boiled over the cliffs and drowned everyone I'd ever known. My family floated atop a lake with hundreds of others, all of them pale and dead and gazing with black eyes to the sunless heavens. My house was but timbers floating in what once had been my father's field.

"Yes," was all I murmured to Hasai. "Veni."

When I think back upon what lay within the old creature's walls, I cannot stifle a shudder. I walked in from the rain, tired and hungry and cold and wet, but my eyes soon widened. Beyond the dry, thousand-cracked front door, I encountered such wonders as I had never seen. The walls were painted with glorious frescos, the rooms stuffed with sculptures of nude maidens and feathered angels, and the floors lined with carpets so soft a man's feet might fall in love. It made no sense to me. How could such things exist inside a cabin atop a cliff? Lithe caryatids kept up the ceiling in his dining room, while the doors to each room were pale and pristine, their surfaces so white I dared not lay my dirty fingers upon them. I had never seen such a collection. I felt I had walked into one of the great cities my father had always rumored about. *But this is just an old man's hovel by the sea,* I remember telling myself. *The sign outside his door says 'Tile Maker'. He should be poor. These walls should be bare. The house should look on the inside the same as it does from without.*

I slept my first night away in a king's bed, my belly full of soup. Hasai awoke me in the morning. When he rolled back the curtains, the sunlight poured into my room like water into a ship's broken hull, and a room full of red frescoes and pale sculptures greeted me. "Your chambers, if you'll have them." Hasai smiled at me. "I've only two rules."

I was such a young, dumb thing. So desperate for a roof over my head and so enchanted by the glorious sights within in the old man's house, I never questioned his offer. "Rules?" I asked him. "Name them. Anything. I need a place to stay. My family is…"

"…dead and gone." Hasai stood in the doorway, old and bald and looking ready to fall to pieces. "Anyhow, the rules. First, no touching the paintings or the sculptures. Look all you like, but run your little grubs along any of them, and I'll send you straight back to Veni."

"No touching." I stared at him, stupid as stone. "Well and good."

"And the second, no leaving your room at night. I've work to do. I won't be disturbed. I'm loud and messy and very, very particular about my work. Do all you like during the day, but if you're not in your room by sunset, you're no guest of mine. It's a prickly rule, I'll admit, but it's mine."

"Well and good," I agreed. "Are the paintings yours?"

"All of them," said Hasai.

"And the sculptures?" I doubted it. No man could be so marvelously skilled.

"See these knobby old fingers?" Hasai made crabs of his hands. "They worked every sculpture here and many others besides."

"The carpets?" I began to believe he was a liar.

"Woven by me, every thread, every knot. Stay with me, boy, and perhaps someday I'll show you how I did it."

I should stop my story now. I should slap my cheek, drink a cup of wine, and teeter down the stairs to where my grandchildren are laughing. My wife would be happy to see me. She says I spend too much time up here. "Glooming." She likes to wag her finger at me. "Always glooming. Come down and sup with us, husband. We've lived long and well, and yet you're glooming."

She is right, of course. But no, I must remember this. I do the same every night. Tonight is no different.

I came to live with Hasai on the outskirts of Tessera. His initial kindness stuck to me in the sort of way I had rarely experienced in Veni. His house atop the cliff was ancient and weathered on the outside, but so like a prince's palace within the walls. He seemed like a father and an uncle all wrapped up into one brittle old body. How could I not trust him? How could I not accept his offer to stay as long as I should like?

On my first morning in his house, he dropped a pouch full of coins into my hand. "Go into Tessera, my lad," he told me. "Spend as you will and make friends with all those you meet. We are a small city, only three and a half hundred. Wander as you like, but return before dark, else out in the wild I'll put you."

I should have thought it odd. *Why, if he's so willing to help, does the old man care when I come and go? It's not as if I mean any harm.*

And yet, like a puppy possessed of a new master, I decided in my heart never to disappoint him. *He will feed me,* I reminded myself. *He offers me a bed with cleaner linens than I've ever known. My room will be warm at night. The walls are covered with paintings of women most men could never dream of. My floors are soft as silk, and in the morning the sun will shine in through my three windows as though happy to see me. I will love this Hasai and treat him as my own grandfather, for he deserves it.*

That morning, I walked into Tessera. My horse had wandered off in the night, and I'd no grief left for him. With my pouch full of coins, I strode down the cliffs and into the city as though it had always been mine. Tessera was a pretty place. Its folk had mined the white rocks right out of the cliffs, polished them to a keen shine, and built up a grand city of the stuff. I saw many thousand houses, all white and clean and with windows open to the sun. Some were full of families, but many others were empty and ready to be

12

moved into. I should have thought the empty houses odd, but instead I remember thinking, *here's a second chance for me. Tessera is everything Veni was not. I hear laughter. I see smiles. People are talking to one another, and not only because they have to, but because they want to. If I fit in here, one of these houses could be mine.*

Hasai's coins bought me all I wanted and more. I breakfasted at the city's only inn, and they were so happy to have a guest they fed me enough for three. They watched me take every bite, topped off my cup with chilled milk whenever I took a sip, and sent me out the door with a sweetloaf under my arm and a belly ready to burst. It was surely the best breakfast I'd ever had.

After breakfast, I wandered down an alley and found myself at a wine-maker's shop. When the owner saw me nosing, he and his pretty daughter led me down to the cellars. The racks were lined with bottles new and old, and the walls stacked with barrels that smelled of trees I'd never had the pleasure to walk beneath. "Two hundred years of making wine for Tessera," the man told me. "But now I've more bottles than I'll ever be able to sell. Your purse is nigh bursting, my friend. Care to buy any?"

"Of course," I said. I'd never had wine before, but I knew I wanted some. I'd heard it could steal a man's sorrows and send him off to dreamless sleeps. I never should have bought the first six bottles. As it happened, deep sleeps were not what I needed.

"How is it you've more bottles than you can sell?" I remember asking the man's daughter as she escorted me back into the sunlight.

"Our customers are all gone." She smiled. I took it for flirtation. I was wrong.

"Gone?"

"Away," she explained. "Gone."

"Oh." I must have sounded like a fool.

After ferrying my bread and bottles back to Hasai's and finding no sign of the old man, I decided to return to Tessera. I'd seen no sunnier day since the storms. The wind off the ocean was warm, the grass swaying like dancing children, and the city so inviting. The more I tasted of Tessera, the more I liked it. People smiled not just for each other; they smiled for me. I must have been a novelty for them. Girls ran out of their houses to walk beside me. Children led me on play chases through the alleys. Wives blew kisses from second-story windows, and husbands stopped their labors just to ask me about me and my life.

I remember one such man. He was a miller, and his hands were powdery white when he came out of his dwelling to greet me. Of all the people I had met, the miller was most interested in how I came to stay at Hasai's. "An old house, that one, the oldest in Tessera," he said when he learned I'd taken a room there.

"Oh?" I asked, stupid again.

"Aye. Two hundred years old, and full o' treasures, they tell. Is it true? I've never been up that cliff in all my life."

"Full of treasure, indeed," I answered. "Sculptures, paintings, and fineries such as I've never seen."

"Well-preserved?" The miller's question was curious.

"Well-maintained," I said. "Clean as if Hasai had made them all yestereve."

The miller shrugged and grinned and gave me a look like my father used to give me when I was a boy. "And you simply made yourself at home? Just unlocked the door and helped yourself?"

"I'm no squatter," I said. "I was invited."

"Invited?" the miller scoffed, but just as quickly turned friendly again. "Well, good on you, lad. I'll not begrudge you being bold and such. Though rare's the man who can sleep in a house so empty."

I should have asked him why he said it, and why he said it the way he did. Alas, me the dunce, I strolled right past his mill and into the fields beyond. *The sun is high. The grass is green,* I remember thinking. *Best not to stay and trouble the miller too long. He'll want to finish his work and take a walk the same as I.*

That eve, I arrived back at Hasai's house in time to keep his second rule. I supped alone at his table until sunset, at which point I took my wine and bread and shut myself in my room. The wine was good, so very good. I slept deeper than the sea beyond the cliffs, and the only sounds I remember were the rain and the old man working into the late hours.

When I awoke the next morn, I found Hasai in the room directly across the hall from mine. He'd torn up the room's carpet in the night, and had begun laying tiles in its place.

"But…" I could barely contain my shock. "The carpet was new. It was soft as grass, the plushest thing I've ever walked on. I know it's not my business, but why would you remove it?"

"You're right, lad." He strained to stand, his bones creaking and cracking. He'd finished laying a single small mosaic of tiles in place, but the bare floor was large enough for several hundred more. "The carpet was wondrous, wasn't it? But I've a new idea in mind. Nobody buys my tiles anymore. They haven't for years. I've lost the art a bit. I'll tile this floor. I'll make a masterpiece, and then I'll be gone."

"You don't mean you'll die, do you?"

"And if I did?" The old man's look sent me scurrying.

Of all the things I remember about Tessera, my first full week is the sharpest. Every morning, I followed the same routine. I breakfasted at the inn, perused the cellars at the winery, ran with the children down the alleys, and talked with girls in the streets. Every day felt sunnier and warmer than the one before it. The rains washing over the cliffs each night left the fields dewy and the streets full of puddles, but under the sun the skies were clear. Every morning was a welcome sight. Every new person I met took me farther from the horrors of home. Every girl I met smiled at me. Every meal I devoured left me satisfied.

And every day, someone in Tessera went missing.

The first day, it was the miller's wife. I remember seeing her watching from the window as her husband and I had conversed. She had been beautiful, and her smile so like the sun upon my cheek. But when I saw the miller for the second time, he brought me inside his home, sat me down at his table, and closed the shutters tight.

"Missing?" I gaped after he'd finished his tale. "I don't understand. I saw her in the window just yesterday. And you say you heard her singing to your daughter just before sundown."

"I know." He looked weary beyond words, well past the point of more tears. "She was, and I did."

"Well…" I stammered. "How is the whole city not searching for her? She could be in one of the empty houses. She could be out in the fields or up on the cliffs. We have to find her, and soon."

The miller did not move. He just sat in his chair, the shadows heavy as storm clouds on his brow. "You've never been to Tessera before, boy. You don't know."

"I still don't understand." I wanted to shake the sense back into him. "She could be out there. She could be alive!"

"She's not. And she isn't." He shook his head at me, and I went silent. "You see all those empty houses out there? You see them? There're thousands, many more empty than full, all white stones and white roofs and white doors. Up until a decade or so ago, they used to be full of families, they did, but Tessera is quiet now, and it must seem to a lad like you that it has always been this way. It hasn't. These streets used to flow with rivers of folk, with merchants from inland, children and old folk and soldiers and such. But now look at it. You see a smile from one window, but you walk past a dozen more before you see another. It's not because you're not

17

worth smiling at. It's because the pretty things who do all the smiling are gone."

"Gone?" I asked the same question as I had of the wine-maker's daughter.

"Missing. Likely dead." The miller told me. "One a day, every day for the last dozen years. Except for yesterday and the day before. We'd hoped you were an omen, we did. But you're not, are you? The others will still smile for you, but not for long."

I could hardly believe it. I shambled back to Hasai's in a stupor. My heart beat faster, but my blood moved slower. I had so many questions, so many shadows in my mind. When the old man proved absent, I drank myself to sleep again. Once more, the rain and Hasai's work on his tiles were all I remembered of the night.

When I walked into Tessera the next morn, I tried to pretend I had not spoken with the miller. The innkeepers all smiled for me, the wine-maker and his daughter sold me a crate at half the normal price, and three lovely girls walked with me as they had the previous day. It was the same every day that week. I followed my routine, and all seemed well. Everyone treated me as though nothing had changed. *The miller was only having fun with me*, I convinced myself. *His wife is perfectly fine. She was only hiding.*

But when I returned to the miller's house on the eighth day, he told me what had happened.

"The tailor." He sat me down at his table again. "The only good one we had, gone in the night, same as my Lilia. And then there's the shepherd, the carpenter, another farmer, and the fisherman's three daughters."

18

"It can't be true," I reasoned. "No one else has said a word."

"And yet here we are," said the miller. "I know you've your doubts. But if you won't believe me, take your questions to the widows, the orphans, and the houses ten years empty. Ask all those who smile for you, and watch their smiles melt away."

I knew right then he was telling the truth. *The orphans are the children who run with me in the streets,* I realized. *The girls who walk with me are the widows, and the empty houses are for whole families gone missing.* "Why doesn't someone do something?" I argued. "And if not, why don't you all leave?"

The miller gave me a sad, sad smile. "No one leaves Tessera, my lad. You think we haven't tried? Ask the jeweler's wife. Her husband fled north to Ellerae years ago, but when she wrote him, she received a letter back from Ellerae's mayor. '*Your husband never arrived, my poor sweet,*' the mayor wrote. '*No one has seen him, same as the last hundred husbands and wives Tessera wrote us about. It's time you and your city stop sending letters. We've seen none of your ghosts. We won't answer you any longer.*'"

"How many are missing?" I did not really want to know.

"Thousands," replied the miller. "One every day."

I did not want to believe it, but in my heart I knew. The next day, my flock of children was one fewer. The day after that, I heard rumors of a woman I'd never met vanishing while washing her clothes at night. The next morn, one of the innkeeper's cousins never came to breakfast. The evening after, a mother found her son's cradle empty. And the next two nights, a pair of brothers who worked in the fields never came home.

After those first two weeks, I still walked down the cliff to visit Tessera every day, but it was a far different experience. No girls walked with me. No one much smiled, save for a few of the children, and our games in the streets soon came to an end. I breakfasted at the inn, but they never topped off my milk or filled my belly to bursting again. It may have been because the milkmaid and the baker had vanished, or it may have been because I wasn't the good omen I was supposed to be. I bought as much wine as I could carry, but a few weeks later, when the wine-maker disappeared, his daughter never again smiled or offered me the bargains her father had.

Autumn descended upon Tessera. The warm spaces between the cold, rainy nights became briefer. To conquer my terror of becoming the next soul to vanish, I became a drunkard. Wine was like water to me. With every glass I swallowed, I felt my mind begin to dull. I awoke with a raging headache each dawn, fearing some horror would be waiting in my room, but Hasai would always knock on my door, offer me tea and a cool towel to wipe away my sweat, and guide me to the kitchen.

"Those poor, poor people." I sat with the old man one morning at the precipice of winter. It was bitterly cold outside his house, and I felt feverish from too much wine. "They've suffered for so long. What must it be like, living under the cloud of death?

And now I'm here. Am I a Tesseran, too? Will I vanish like all the others?"

Hunkered like a pile of old bones in his chair, Hasai shook his head. "It's best not to think about it, my lad."

"Not think about it?" I raved. "How could I?"

"Become my apprentice."

"How will that help?"

"Hard work has a way of walling off the heart." He folded his puny, skeletal fingers together. "And as you've lived under my roof for so long, it's time you repaid me."

The old man was right. I owed him. I had supped at his table, spent his coins, wandered drunk through his hallways, and soaked in the warmth of his hearth, all of it without working. In hindsight, I suppose it was guilt that made me begin my apprenticeship. I didn't want to work, to be certain. I wanted to pile seven layers of clothes on my shoulders and stride down the cliff to discover who Tessera's latest loss had been.

But no, I stayed. I helped him. I'll never forgive myself.

For seven months, we worked every day. He forbade me my daily jaunts to Tessera, and although I hated him for it, after several weeks I came to understand it was better that way. I drank far less. I forgot my fears. I worked from dawn until dusk, and just as he promised, the walls around my heart grew higher. I began to forget Tessera. I cast the miller's wife, the wine-maker, the little boy I used to run with, and all the rest of them out of mind.

In the first few weeks, it was mortar for his sculptures he ordered me to make. In the chamber behind his kitchen, he'd pour white grit into a tub and I'd mix it with rain we'd collected in buckets or melted snow we'd sloughed off the eaves. I stirred and stirred and stirred, until the stuff broke down into a pale, viscous fluid. I can't recall how many tubs I churned for him. Hundreds? A thousand? What I remember most is climbing into bed each night, my forearms afire and my fingernails crusted over with sticky white paste.

After the mortar, we came to the paint-making. He'd already described the dozens of frescoes he wanted to create. He desired to scroll his walls with fierce, feminine angels locked in battle with hosts of underworld horrors. "Where will you put them?" I remember asking. "Your walls are painted already." But he'd just flash his yellow teeth and say, "I'll paint over the others. Old art is tired. It's new art, fresh and fine, that'll line these walls once I'm gone from Tessera."

As he bid, I toiled. He'd bring in a few buckets of yellows and blues for blending, but it was mostly the reds he had me make. The reds are what I remember best. I hated the scarlet paint, its thickness, and its smell. He'd give me oils to change the consistency and strange inks to add or steal color, but it made no difference. I'd ask every day, "Might I drink some wine while I do this?" But he'd always wag his bony finger at me and say, "You've drank enough, I think, and all with my coin. Fret not, my lad. At the end, you'll have all to drink you could ever hope for."

I never stopped to think about why.

Winter floated past. Spring fluttered by. Summer returned. It rained or snowed every night during my stay at Hasai's, but never so much as during the hot season. The storms roiled over the cliffs, threatening to tear the world in two. Had I not been so exhausted by grinding, pouring, mixing, sanding, hauling, and the hundreds of other chores the old man made me perform, I might have been afraid. As it was, I'd forgotten how to worry. *If I haven't vanished yet, I never will,* I told myself. And since I'd not been back to Tessera in months, I dreamed in my head the disappearances had stopped.

Then one day during summer's end, Hasai woke me. I was bleary, hungry, and in want of a storm to sweep the old man's house into the sea, *and with me in it.* He took me to the room across the hall, the very one he had kept locked since that first morn he showed me his new tiles.

That day remains as crisp as any in my mind. As I sit in my room with the moonlight pooling on my table, I feel sick with the memory. I can hear my grandchildren laughing, and it remains my one joy in life that they know none of what happened in Tessera. My children do, of course, and my bride. But they never truly believed me. They heard the rumors from a hundred folk besides me, and they have long reasoned it was the plague that took Tessera. *But what about the other cities?*

Hasai hobbled into the room across the hall. I walked in behind him. It took me a moment for my bleariness to fade, but when it did, I saw he'd finished the floor. I'd never seen such beauty. The mosaic of tiles made music for my eyes. My mouth hung open, and I stared as though a dozen angels had disrobed for my pleasure. "You finished it," I said, still as stupid as ever.

"One mosaic a day." The old man grinned at me, his teeth rotting in his mouth. "One hundred tiny tiles in each one."

"How many mosaics in the room?" I wondered.

"Three hundred sixty."

"Oh."

I walked across the floor barefooted. They were angels I stepped upon, bright and bold as sunshine, warring with hosts of shadows. I saw the simple chores I'd performed come at last to fruition. Bright reds made up the angels' swords. Pale, perfect white mortar sealed the tiny lines between each tile. The glues I had made were surely at rest beneath the entire floor, holding the mosaics in place. The blacks I had blended gave the demons life.

"It's perfect." I remember drawing a breath after holding it for a long while.

Hasai let me stand there until I'd taken it all in. Later, as we breakfasted in the kitchen, he pushed me a purse of coins. It was fatter than all the others he'd given me, and full of gold instead of silver.

"I don't deserve this," I told him. It was true. I didn't.

"Take it to Tessera, my lad." Hasai smiled one last smile. "Buy whatever you like in the world. You've earned your keep. You've helped me finish my masterpiece. And now it's time for me to sleep."

"You don't mean die, do you?" I still hate myself for the tear that dribbled down my cheek.

"And if I do?"

"Where'd you earn all this gold?" I was still so young, still so foolish. "You've had no customers all year. All the sculptures and paintings we made are still here, still in the house."

"So they are," said Hasai. "And so they shall remain."

That was the last thing I ever heard him say. He wandered off behind the kitchen, and I departed for Tessera shortly thereafter. The walk down the cliff was longer than I remembered. It had rained the previous night, and the ground was soft and squelching. I can hardly believe I had forgotten poor Tessera. All the truths the miller had told me had leaked out of my simple little head. To think I set foot on those streets, my bag full of money and my heart soaring with pride for what I'd helped create. I'm as much to blame as Hasai.

So there I was, striding through the heart of Tessera. Its emptiness washed over me in the same way the storms had in Veni. I suppose I knew even then, but I pretended otherwise. I walked to the inn, but no one was there. The door swayed in the summer wind, and a half-eaten meal lay rotting atop a table. I noticed the windows were shuttered and barred. I saw a sword lying naked on the floor. *Someone tried to hide here*, I knew. *But someone else came for them.*

Still too foolish to be afraid, I wandered the rest of the city. No children ran along the streets. I found a pair of empty sandals in a gutter and a pile of crates stacked high in an alley where the little ones used to meet, but I heard none of their laughter. When I fled to the wine-maker's house, I hoped against hope to

25

see the pretty girl. I'd have married her, I would, if she'd have had me, but it was a false hope. I battered my way through a side door and descended into the shadows of the cellar. I found rotting bread, a block of moldy cheese, and other evidence that the poor girl had holed herself away in the darkest corner. But she was gone, and Hasai had been right. If I had wanted it, all the wine in the world was waiting for me to drink.

Terror began to work its way into my blood. I fled to the miller's house. *He was the sanest one*, I told myself. *He knew more than he told me. I should have listened.* His house was one of few without its windows barred and its doors barricaded. His daughter was gone and so was he. Whatever had come for him, he'd let it take him without a fight. He'd known. *There was no escape, not for anyone.*

I roamed like a vagabond from street to street, calling out the names and professions of the people I had known. I screamed for the candy-maker, the glass-blower, the piper, the carpenter's widow, the blacksmith's son, the farmer's cousin, and even the whore. I loped from door to door, banging my fist against them until I bled. I shattered windows and crashed through planks of wood, but every house was the same, much as they had been during my first day in Tessera. I heard no sounds but the rats squeaking. I saw no evidence of struggles. Everyone was gone. I knew in my heart they were not missing. I knew they had been taken.

At dusk, after my desperate, fruitless search, I ran back up the cliff. I was delirious. I hadn't eaten or sipped any wine since breakfast. My heart was a frozen hammer wailing against my rocklike ribs, near to shattering me with every stroke. As I pelted up the rocks, I worried that Hasai would shut me out of his house. *The darkness is here,* I told myself. *I've broken his rule.*

His door was open. I had expected it to be locked. In a panic, I ran through the house, screaming, "Hasai! Hasai! Help!" The statues and paintings which had seemed so magnificent by day leered at me in the dusklight. They looked alive, the angels' eyes judging me, the demons hungry to stretch my skin. Into all of the house's nine rooms I burst, but the old man occupied none of them. It only then occurred to me I'd never seen a bed besides my own. *Where does he sleep?* I asked myself. *My bed is the only one in the house.*

I fled into the kitchen. The table was exactly as I'd left it. My breakfast, only half-eaten, remained. Drunk with panic and startled by the sounds of rain beginning to clatter against the roof, I pushed into the room behind the kitchen, a place I'd rarely gone.

And there I found the door.

I dream often about the door. I fantasize about what my life would have been had I not opened it. Maybe I'd have walked away from Tessera with my bag of gold and been none the wiser. I'd have known something had gone horribly awry, but not the why and how of it. When I placed my bloodied palm on that dry, dusty plank of oak and pushed, my life and the lives of everyone I've met since that night changed.

I was such a fool. Down the stairs I walked and into the cellars beneath the cliffs. I heard the wind, the rain, and the sea slashing against the walls. I found a lantern. I never remembered how I stoked its light to life, but I did.

Hasai's dungeon lay before me.

I saw crates, each one with a name. Some were empty, but others were stuffed with bones. I saw the wine-maker's crate and beside it his daughter's. The pretty hat she used to wear lay within, sitting atop her skull. Her father's bones jutted over the rim of his crate. Half of each one was missing. I saw a device made of steel lying near. *For shaving the bones.* My heart stopped and restarted when I realized it. *For making powder. For making mortar.*

I went mad with terror. I ran to each crate, calling out the names. I saw children's crates, the innkeepers' crates, the miller, his daughter, and his wife's crates. All the pretty widows were there, right beside their husbands. I saw jars with black fluid in some and pouches stuffed with bone dust in others. The dank, stone walls sheltered all the dead Hasai had ever collected. *Thirteen years' worth*, I knew. *One a day, every day.*

I feared the monster would find me. Lost in his network of chambers, I fled for the door, but instead came to the old horror's workbench. *His art,* I knew when I saw the surgeon's saws, the black tubes, glass phials, and other instruments of dissection. *No. No, no, no. Please help me. His art, his art, his art.*

I knew then I'd helped him. The red paint, the mortar, the fluids, the smells, the oils, the glue, and all the rest had come from Tessera's people. The canvases for his paintings were skins. The carpets were spun of maidens' hair. The statues of nude girls were not statues at all, but humans preserved by some manner of madness. His paints were Tessera's insides, his tiles made of carefully carved bone. Hasai's house was an exhibit, and he was its ghoulish artist, a demon in an old man's skin. No human could have cleaned out the city with such morbid efficiency, I knew. No feeble sack of bones possessed the power to overtake grown men without a struggle. One by one, the unholy creature had sniffed them out and stolen them away. No matter where they'd run, he had chased them down and tore their lives away in the silence of the night. *And he'd done it all while I lay to sleep in his house, drunk and dreaming of the poor dead women locked in sculpture all around me.*

I ran howling from the house, from Tessera, from the world. I still had his bag of gold tethered to my waist. Where I went and how I survived all those nights in the bitter rain, I'll never be able to piece together. Hasai never came for me, but he'd killed me all the same. I've wondered ever since if the angels he'd painted were the Tesserans, and himself the demons made of shadow.

And so here I am, still breathing, but dead inside. I sit alone in my study. My grandchildren have gone quiet and my wife has stopped asking for me to come to bed. My lamp long ago burned out, but the moonlight remains. Only two things rest on my table. One is the pouch Hasai gave me. A few golden coins remain within, a small fortune to most men. They are Tesseran, these coins. I earned none of them. If Hasai was one monster, I am the other. I spent Tessera's gold to buy this house, these clothes, the ring on my wife's finger, and a thousand suppers besides. All I own is lies. All I am is stolen.

The other item atop my table is a list. *Tessera,* the curled up sheaf of paper says. *Milici, Catani, Polera, Ellerae.* They are the names of cities. Tessera, Milici, Catani, and Polera are all dead anymore. They say the plague killed everyone years ago, but then, the plague has been gone for half a century. It was no disease that emptied these places. Go to any one of them, and you'll find no graves. It was Hasai who cleaned them out. Give the old ghoul enough time, and he'll make a mural of all the world.

It's raining tonight. The street lamp beyond my window hisses and dies. It's autumn in Ellerae, and the rain is hardly unusual, but I know the truth of it. It has rained every night for the last thirty. People have started to go missing.

One a night. Every night, I tell myself. *Until everyone is gone.*

Let the Bodies

Hello.

My name is Mia.

I'm a little girl, or at least sometimes I still *pretend* I am.

I used to live in Ellerae, a stone's toss from Lake Po.

Ellerae was the most beautiful city in the world, so says everyone who's ever been there. We had blue waters in the south and white mountains to the north. We had olive trees everywhere. We had vineyards, farms, and orchards, too. Everything was green and blue and white. Everywhere I looked: trees, water, and pale stones.

I *loved* Ellerae. I didn't ever want to leave.

My first memories of living there are of our old stone house on Osso Street. I lived with Grandpa and Grams in a tall, skinny, three-story house. The bottom two floors were bricked with river stones, and the top story made of old oak planks hammered together with rusty nails. All the houses looked the same on Osso. '*Thin as switches*,' Grandpa used to say. '*Older than the rocks they're built of. A missing brick and a half-hearted kick from falling right over.*'

That never made much sense to little me, but then again lots of what Grandpa used to say confused me. He was all sayings, all the time. He had proverbs for everything, like, '*Wine's good for sleeping, but bad for waking,*' and, '*Never eat a noodle that won't stick to the bricks.*'

I guess what mattered is that we were happy in our skinny house. We loved it even when it sagged with all the others. We loved it in winter, when the hearth would roar and warm us like a second sun. And we loved it in summer when the vines crept up the walls and the rain drummed on the shingles all night long.

I loved Grams especially.

For as much as Grandpa was all sayings, riddles, and stories of the old world, Grams was rooted in hard truths and harder work. While Pa smoked his pipe and sipped himself clumsy with his wine, Grams baked us bread, swept the floors, scrubbed our dirty clothes, and walked to markets near and far to fetch makings for supper. We always used to think she'd be upset with Pa for his glooming, smoking, and lazing about. But no, she never was, leastways not that she'd let us see.

"You work so hard, but not *Pa*," I remember my little brother Gio saying to Grams one morning while Grandpa was away. "How come?"

"Your Pa's worked hard enough," she said while sweeping.

"Is it 'cause he's got all the coins?" Gio blurted. "Cousin Sully says if you have lots of coins, you don't have to work."

Grams laughed at that. "Maybe that's true. Maybe a little."

"Why?" I butted in.

"Well…Gio's right." Grams stopped sweeping. "Not because of what Sully said. But because Pa's coins let us live this life. Without the coins, we'd have to work harder. I'd be out in the fields. Pa would be at the mill, or maybe the cobblers, or maybe slaving long shifts at the tannery. Life wouldn't be as simple."

"Did Ma and Da work at those places?" Gio asked. "Is that why they're gone?"

"Gio—" I scolded him.

"No, it's a fair question," Grams sighed. "Truth is…I'm not sure why your Ma and Da left. I think Pa knows, but it's not his favorite thing to talk about. '*Scared of their own shadows*,' Pa used to say. Though I don't hardly know what he meant. Not really, anyway."

Gio thought on it for a moment. He was only five winters along, '*but already smarter than sunshine*,' Pa always liked to say. "How'd he get all the coins?" my little brother asked. "He's got big piles upstairs. More coins than everyone on Osso, all added up."

Maybe it was the way Grams stopped sweeping, or maybe it was the quick shadow flooding her eyes, but I knew just then Gio had asked the right question. Or maybe he'd asked the *wrong* one, and I was too dumb to know the difference.

"Gio, dear," said Grams, "you've finished your breakfast. I think it's time you went to play. The cold snaps will be here in a few weeks. Not many more days as pretty as this."

"Awwww, but *Grams*—" he complained.

"Run along." She managed a smile. "Be back for supper. I'll have pie for you. You too, Mia. Until dusk, you're to play. Come back tired and dirty, else no pie."

"But *Grams*—" I echoed my brother's protest.

"*Apple* pie," she said. "Your *favorite*. Now *go*."

I couldn't argue with apple pie. Neither of us could. We dashed out the door and played all day. Just as Grams had hoped, we came back at dusk, and neither of us remembered to ask about the coins.

In a few weeks came autumn.

And in a few weeks more, winter.

The seasons were like that in Ellerae. Springs and autumns were quick as sparrows flying past the window. But summers and winters were like old men shambling down the road. The hots and colds were slow and seemed to last forever. Summers were long. Winters felt like eternities.

I suppose we never much minded. With Pa's coins, we never wanted for anything. Which was good, I guess. Until it wasn't.

It was during the coldest day that winter I wandered up to Pa's room on the top floor. The downstairs was flooded with family. Cousin Sully had died a few days prior, and every relative in Ellerae had turned out to mourn and '*eat all our pie*,' as Gio had realized. I couldn't stand the crush of family pinching my cheeks, talking about how tall and pretty I'd grown, or how pale the winter had made me. I preferred the quiet of Pa's old and oaky study. I liked the way his pipe's smoke filled the whole room.

When I cracked his door open and crept inside, I found him sitting beside his biggest window, staring onto the street below.

"Hi, Pa." My voice was barely a whisper. I wasn't sure if he'd be upset with me invading his privacy.

"Come in, Mia." He glanced at me. His cheeks were red and his eyes glazed. I knew right away he'd been sipping wine.

I sidled across the room and propped my elbows on his desk. I saw what he'd been staring at: a white streetlamp blazing beneath the window.

"When Ellerae goes dark," he murmured, "our little streetlamp is always the last one burning. It's the same every night. All the others go out, but ours stays lit. Funny how that is."

I looked out the window again. Dusk was settling and Ellerae going dark. Snow dusted every roof on Osso, while the clouds, greyer than Pa's beard, scudded across the sky. Sure enough, our streetlamp burned steady. It looked like a little moon, paling the cobblestones and making shadows dance on the houses' sides.

"It's pretty," I remarked.

"Maybe so." Pa looked at me. "Reminds me of home. We had one lamp just like it in Veni. Just *one*. After the storms came, it was the only thing left standing."

I suppose I should've caught the sadness in his eyes. Thinking back on it, I can see it clear as day.

"*What* storms, Pa?" I asked.

"The ones that took Veni away," he sighed. "They were strange, those storms. They came from the sea *and* the mountains. From all directions, it felt like. And when they were finished with us, the streetlamp was the only thing left. Even when I trotted away on the last living horse, the post was still standing…and a little fire flickering behind the glass. But nothing else survived. Not a stone. Not a brick. Not a single crooked plank. It was all gone, all washed out to sea. Like the ghosts had come to take everything away. Everything but me."

I was old enough to allow a solemn silence to pass. Only after we looked out the window for a long while did I dare speak again. For the life of me, I can't say why I decided to ask him what I did.

"Pa, where'd you get all your coins?"

"In the city by the cliffs." He looked out the window. "A *big* city. A *beautiful* city. They didn't need their money anymore, so I helped myself."

"Oh," I exhaled.

"Aye," he puffed. "And just like Veni and just like here, there was a streetlamp. I remember it now. It burned at the city's edge. A pretty little light, yellow and fierce. Same as Veni, it was the last thing I saw when I left."

"Oh," I said again. "What was the city called?"

"Tessera."

I shrugged. I'd never heard of such a place. Sure, there'd been stories about Veni, but never one about a beautiful city by the sea.

I suppose I should've asked Pa more.

I didn't.

The next morning, I clomped downstairs from my bed and sank into the chair next to Gio. It didn't much matter that a snowstorm was howling outside. Gio looked as sunny as ever in his life.

"What are *you* so cheery about?" I asked him.

"Auntie Lessa gave me a present. If you'd been downstairs, you'd have got one, too," he declared.

"I'd have got one what?"

"A ring!" He beamed and hoisted a slender golden band up for me to see. I tried to grab it, but apparently he being *two* years younger made him *ten* years faster. "It's mine!" He grinned stupidly. "Auntie says it was Sully's. When I'm bigger, it'll fit me. Auntie says it'll protect me from *everything*. And if I wear it, I'll live *forever*."

I couldn't have rolled my eyes farther back even if I'd tried. "You're so dumb," I blurted. "If it protected Sully from everything, why'd he go and die?"

"They don't know he's dead." Gio made a face. "He's just *missing*."

"Missing five days. In winter. Face it, Gio; his bones are powder by now. He's probably blowing around with the snow, *ooooo oooooooooooooo*!" I made a sound like a groaning ghost.

"That's enough, Mia," Grams scolded. "You'll scare him."

As she ladled breakfast mash into my bowl, I sank deeper into my chair. "Scare Gio?" I grumped. "Not hardly. He knows all about dead people. There was uncle Vin last year, and Brick-maker Lupa, and Cobbler Sams, and—"

"Yes, dear," Grams said mildly. "Now eat your mash."

Completely jealous of Gio's ring, I nibbled at my breakfast. It was salty, just the way I liked it. Grams had never made a bad meal in her life. Her food tasted like love. No wonder Pa had married her.

And the longer I sat there, trying to be mad, the more Gio's smiles wore me down. I couldn't stay angry with him. No chance. He kept sticking his tongue out at me and giggling. And when he crossed his eyes and balanced his spoon on his nose, I burst out laughing.

"You noodle." I rolled my eyes again, though not half as far back. "When you're done with your mash, I'll hold you up by your ankles and pour it all back out of you. Right out your nose, it'll drip. *Bloop, bloop, bloop!*"

And we laughed again.

And finished our breakfast.

And played inside our skinny house all day long.

If I'd tears left, I'd cry. But I can't. Not anymore.

Because that day was the last I ever spent with Gio.

I remember waking up a few days after he disappeared. I sat there in the predawn gloom, listening to the wind howl, waiting for my little brother to pounce out of the darkness and start tickling me. I held my breath for what felt like hours. *He's coming,* I convinced myself. *He's been hiding all this while. It's just a game for him. Any moment now, he'll jump on the bed and we'll cuddle until Grams calls us down for breakfast.*

But he never pounced. Never laughed. Never tickled me ever again.

Twenty-three days after he vanished, Grams called for another mourning. It was like Sully's, only quieter and without any pie. People had talked during Sully's. They'd told stories about him, about the nutty things he used to claim, and about all his silly superstitions.

But at Gio's mourning, no one much talked at all. Pa didn't even come home for it. 'Too heartbroken,' Grams wept. 'First his children, now *this*.'

As I sat in the darkness of Pa's oaky study, Grams came up with a candle. I couldn't ever remember seeing her in that room before. And I don't think she ever came up again.

"Mia, you should come down. The other children…they're worried."

I looked out the window. Evening was drawing down, and the pale streetlamp was already burning. Come to think of it, I didn't recall seeing anyone lighting its little fire.

"They're not *worried*," I mumbled to Grams. "They're *scared*."

Grams stood beside me. "Why should they be scared, dearie? This was an accident. It's not as though—"

"…it'll happen again?" I finished her sentence. "But that's just it, Grams. It *might*. Gio's not the first, you know. A few weeks ago, it was Lito. And last autumn, Alesio. And that little girl, Rosie. And that's just the children."

"You sound like Sully's family," Grams gloomed.

"Well maybe they're right." I cupped my chin in my palm. "Maybe we should move to the countryside like the Angelos did. Or the Bruenis. I like Ellerae and all, but—"

Grams hugged me then. I tried to resist her. I really did. But after a while my tears broke and I started sobbing. All my reason, logic, and fear flew out the window and burned up in the streetlamp's flame. All I could think of was Gio, and the giant hole in my heart he'd left behind.

For two years that felt like two hundred, I kept to myself.

Sure, I went to school. I breakfasted with Grams and went to Auntie Lessa's and tried to play with the other children. I went fishing on Lake Po, shopped at market with our neighbors, and talked whenever spoken to. But it didn't matter anymore. Nothing really did. I knew Gio wasn't coming back. I hoped, but I knew. Whenever I lay in bed alone, which was far too often, I felt it way deep down inside. I'd never known how huge a part of me he had been. Without a real mother and father, he'd been my truest family. He'd been more than Grams, more than Pa, more than all the rest of the world put together.

Two years, and nothing.

As I wallowed through the summers and hid myself away during the winters, things changed in Ellerae. I didn't pay much attention, of course. I was lost in my own head, present in body but otherwise a ghost. Should I have listened to all that happened? Yes. Did I? No. Not really. When Auntie Lessa vanished, I barely batted an eyelash. When four more children from school didn't come home, I was the only one who didn't cry. When Grams hobbled into the house after going to market, she'd murmur about a farmer disappearing, a wife gone missing, or a whisper of a rumor of shadows in the alleys stealing one life every night.

But I barely heard it.

Even though I didn't much listen, Grams told me everything. About life. About death. About everything. If I think hard about it, I know why she chose me to talk to. I know why she came to my room instead of Pa's. He wasn't around much, after all. *Off drinking*, I presumed. *Hiding away with the other old men. Gambling and grumbling about how Ellerae was falling to pieces.*

Grams just wanted someone to talk to.

But I was deaf to it.

I felt like a nine year-old going on ninety. I felt old. Sad. Bitter.

That winter, when Osso Street finally went on curfew because of the vanishings, I must've been the only kid who didn't care. *It's not so bad,* I told myself. *It's quieter this way. I won't have to pretend to play anymore.* The curfew started two days after the Issepe Twins went missing during a trip to their uncle's vineyard. One vanished on the first night. The second disappeared the very next. The whole street must've cried their eyes out. But not me. *Why didn't they just come home after the first night?* I remember thinking while Grams was sniffling about the whole thing. *Could've saved at least one of them.*

It was the last time in my life I wished I'd had Ma and Da back.

For just one winter night, I let myself think about them. I didn't much remember my parents, not anymore, but even so, I fantasized about them coming back. I imagined they were strong and brave and able to help me shut the rest of the world out. With them in my head, I dreamed of a better life. No crying. No empty days and emptier nights. Just me, them, and Gio, together and happy.

It wasn't that I didn't love Grams anymore.

I did. I *really* did. But she hadn't protected Gio. And for that, both she and Pa had become less to me.

Come a night at winter's end, I broke curfew.

I couldn't be in the house anymore. Not that night. Grams had cooked and accidentally set out a plate for Gio. Afterward she'd burst into tears, and Pa had slunk out the back door again. Not that I could blame him for it. The house was too quiet, too *dead*. I needed a walk. I needed to get away.

So, even knowing I'd get in trouble, I walked up and down Osso Street twice. The darkness was heavy. The snow was deep and cold, but I barely felt it. I wore my boots and mittens, and yet some part of me knew that even if I'd gone out in nothing but my skin, I'd have been fine. No one was awake, of course. *Locked behind their doors.* I shook my head. *Afraid of ghosts.*

I don't know why, but I wasn't afraid. Not even a little. *Not my night to vanish*, I knew.

When I came up the street a second time and saw a woman weeping beneath our streetlamp, I wasn't even startled.

"What's the matter?" I walked up to her.

Kneeling in the snow, she looked up at me, but said nothing. Her bare hands were whiter than the moon, her eyes glazed with tears half turned to icicles.

"Can I help?" I asked. It felt compassionate at the time, but in truth it might've been the stupidest question I'd ever asked.

"No," she sobbed. "No help. Not for me."

"It's safe, you know," I blurted. "Someone's already gone missing today. The little boy at Osso's end. Didn't you hear? You don't have to be afraid."

She looked at me again. Her eyes were as blue as Lake Po, her sorrow twice as deep. After a breath, my heart sank into my boot bottoms. *Oh God,* I thought. *She's his mother.*

I tried to speak. I couldn't. The night air froze my lips together, or was it the cold in the woman's eyes? She stood up and squared my shoulders in her frostbitten hands. I swear I almost died.

"You shouldn't be out here," she said through her chattering teeth. "Of all the places in Ellerae, not *here* especially."

"What do you mean, not *here*?"

She clutched my shoulders so hard it hurt. She looked so wild and full of terror in her heartbreak, I thought for a moment she meant to shake me to pieces. But instead she glanced up at the streetlamp and shook her head like a slow, sad pendulum.

"The streetlamp." She shivered. "Glows colder every night. You watch it, little girl. It'll burn brighter tomorrow. And when it finally gets *you*, it'll burn brightest of all."

43

She released my shoulders and staggered away into the darkness. My fearlessness dried up. Quaking, I fled back inside and took every word of Grams' wrath without saying a word.

For many nights afterward, I hid in my room. Even when Grams decided I'd been punished enough for breaking curfew, I stayed behind my door. I ate supper on my bed. I made fortresses of Gio's old blocks and towers using my stuffed dolls. Grams understood, I think. She sang songs through the keyhole, pushed sheaves of paper for me to draw on under the door, and traded me candles for dirty dishes whenever I finished supper. I loved her for it. But not enough to come out. Because I knew the parts she left out of her songs. *People are still disappearing. She just doesn't want to tell me.*

On the first day of spring, Pa finally came for me. I knew it was him by the boom of his heavy boots on the stairs.

"Mia," he said, gruffer than ever I'd heard him. "Mia, come out."

I floated to the door. My white dress was dirty, my socks covered in cobwebs, and my eyes haunted. When I opened the door and saw him standing there, I was terrified of what he'd think.

"You haven't seen the sun in weeks," he grunted at me. "It'll forget you, Mia. It'll lose you."

"It already has," I murmured.

He grinned faintly. "No. Not yet, it hasn't. Your time'll come, sure enough. But for now you've still got mortar between your bricks. Now come upstairs with me. I've something to show you."

If I think about it, really think about it, I should've stayed in my room. I should've shut the world out and waited for everyone else in Ellerae to vanish.

I should've let Pa go on his way. Alone.

But I didn't.

On skinny, wavering legs, I wobbled up the stairs and into Pa's oaky chambers. Clouds of pale dust greeted my footfalls, and shadows danced on the walls. The whole place stank of something, though I wasn't sure what. I'd been certain it had been dawn when Pa had knocked on my door, but the pallid light glooming through the window told me that dusk was near, *and that the streetlamp is burning*.

"I tried. Oh I tried, I did," Pa rambled senselessly while scrabbling around on his big table.

"Tried what, Pa?" I asked.

"To be a good man. To live a good life. To earn it. These damnable coins."

"I don't understand, Pa."

"Course not." He knocked over an urn and dumped an armload of musty books off a shelf. He was beet red and breathing heavily. I just stood in the doorway, frozen.

"Gio, Gio, Gio," he popped a crate open and flipped it over on the floor. "Why'd it have to be Gio? As punishment? To make my end of the bargain hurt more? And you, sweet Mia. We might as well be dead. All of us. All for these damn coins."

I'd never been so scared in my life. Somehow, I found the courage to take three steps into the room. I saw what had been in the crate. *Coins,* I stared at them. *Thousands of coins.*

Pa had more coins than ever we'd guessed.

He scooped hundreds into a sack and thrust them into my arms. I thought I'd collapse under the weight. They were so heavy, heavier than they should have been.

"Take them," he commanded. "All of them. Buy a horse, a coat, and a big bag of food. Ride north. Into the mountains, Mia. Don't go south, whatever you do. Stay away from the lake."

I just stood there, arms sagging. "Pa, I'm scared. What are you saying? I don't understand."

"You have to ride. It's the only way. I know what you're thinking, sweetie. It's not *permanent*. You're still *doomed*. But maybe with the coins, you'll last longer. Maybe even the *longest*. Worked for me. All these years, one every day, and I'm still here."

My fear turned to confusion. Pa was making no sense. His riddles had filled him up to the top of his head. He'd lost his mind.

"Pa, I can't leave. I can't. You're never here. Grams needs me."

He gripped my arm and squeezed. It hurt so bad, I winced. Some of the coins fell out and clattered on the floor. "You...*have*...to," he growled. "If you don't, nothing in Ellerae can help you. My time's up, don't you see? Might be the coins buy you a few years. Might not. But you have to try."

He stared a hole right through me. I felt like shallow water under the summer sun, steaming with the heat. But inside I was frozen solid. No matter how hard he looked at me and willed me to see his madness, I couldn't thaw. And he knew it.

I suppose I should've listened to him and ridden away.

But I didn't.

Pa left that night. I knew I'd probably never see him again. He didn't take any coins. He didn't throttle me and make me promise to flee the city. He just walked downstairs and out the front door. If he said anything to Grams, I didn't hear it. Nor did I ask her.

I hid the coins under my bed. The bag was full to bursting, but I shoved it back into the corner where the sun never shined. Thousands more of the little silver discs sat on Pa's oaky floor, but those I didn't touch. I left them right where they'd fallen. *The only thing that'll touch them is the dust*, I told myself. *I don't want them. I've nothing to spend them on.*

After Pa left, Grams and I were all who remained in the house. I didn't go to school anymore. It didn't matter. Half the kids had vanished. Half the teachers, too. We left the house only to get food and supplies, and then we scurried home, bolted the door shut, and lived in the shadows.

No matter that nearly all our hours were spent locked away, we heard. We listened to the shouts in the street. We read the news rags slipped under our door. We heard the mutters at market. And we saw the toll the hours were taking.

One missing every night.
For seventy years.
No one who leaves is ever heard from again.
No bodies found.
Ever.
People hoped it would stop.
But everyone knew it wouldn't.

Every night after Grams went to sleep, I went up to Pa's room. I knew I shouldn't have. I knew nothing good would come of it. But even so, I did it. It's not like I could've slept. It's not as if Pa would've come back and made everything better. In truth, I just wanted to watch the streetlamp. I wanted to see if it'd get a little brighter each night.

And sure enough, it did.

It must've been another year that passed. I can't really remember it now. My ritual was the same every eve: eat supper with Grams, sing her to sleep, clean up the kitchen, and slink up to the window in Pa's room. It was so quiet. The world felt empty, and little me the only person left alive. Long after dusk, I'd sit in Pa's ancient chair and gaze through the glass. There stood the streetlamp, its light as bright as the world ending. No one ever lit it.

But somehow, it burned.

And then one night, as I sat there with darkness in my eyes, I saw someone walk beneath the lamp. A man, old and bent, shouldered his way through the shadows and stopped in the pool of pale radiance. My bones went cold inside me. My jaw felt frozen, my blood like ice. The man might've been Pa, might not have been. He had Pa's old hat and brown smoking jacket, but the way he walked was different. He was hunched. His bones were all wrong.

And as he stood there in the light, waiting for something, he looked up at me.

To this day I can't remember what I saw.

The next morning, dark rumors swirled at market. A sad woman murmured that the city guard, or at least what was left of them, had found an old

48

house at city's edge. In the house, they'd uncovered three floors worth of art. They'd found sculptures, rare tiles, and rotting rugs. They'd found paintings of people who'd never lived in Ellerae. But that wasn't what scared everyone. What had everyone all aquiver was that the guards had also found tools, as in *mortuary* tools. They'd found boxes of scalpels, bone saws, chisels, needles, and butcher knives. All of it had been mixed in with the art. Tools. Hundreds of tools.

Worse yet, they'd found that all the art had been made of *people*. The sculptures weren't made of marble or clay, but of hollowed-out humans covered in plaster. The rugs were woven of skin, the paintings drizzled with blood and viscera, and the tiles fashioned of graven bones. They even found little mounds of white powder, *bone powder*, the leftovers from whatever horrors had taken place. Whoever had lived in the house had long vanished, but the grisly remains were still there.

"They wanted us to find it," the sad woman cursed the house. "They wanted us to be afraid."

"Who?" someone else asked.

But no one could answer.

I wasn't surprised. I wasn't even terrified. I wasn't curious. I wasn't *anything*.

I just remembered what Pa had said: *'Might be the coins buy you time. Might not.'*

Days later, a few hundred folk gathered up every horse, carriage, and blanket in the city. In a huge procession, they took the south road toward the fields beyond Lake Po. I wanted to watch them leave, if only to know whether some horror scooped them up

49

or whether they got away just fine, but Grams wouldn't let me. "Stay behind locked doors, Mia," she scolded me. "Stay, stay, stay. Nothing can hurt us here. It's all a lie. A sweet, terrible lie."

She'd lost her mind, same as Pa, only worse.

But maybe she was right not to let me watch.

Because the next day when they sent an outrider to see if the procession had made it south, the mayor's man found only riderless horses, empty carriages, and beds that had been made but never slept in.

Gone. All of them...gone.

And the next night, the mayor vanished, too.

For another year and many months, we stayed in our old house. We snuck out only for food and water, though often we'd go without both. *Maybe*, I hoped, *the coins will protect us. Or maybe we'll be the last to go missing.* During that awful time, I many times thought to take Pa's coins and flee north like he'd told me. But I couldn't leave Grams. She needed me. Her mind was empty anymore, and most of the work had fallen on my skinny little shoulders. Besides, with all the horses gone and most of the farmers missing, I'd never make it far. No horses meant I'd have to walk the mountain passes on foot. And no farmers meant no extra food for me to take.

So we stayed. And we survived. One by one, the houses on Osso went empty. Some people vanished in the night like all the rest. Others tried to walk the southern road and were never heard from again. It became comforting, in a way. After that year and a half, Grams and I were the only ones left on the whole street. There was no curfew anymore. There was no one to enforce it. And so Osso became mine. I raided every cupboard, pilfered every toy, and snatched every knickknack. I turned our silent house into a museum, though sometimes it felt like a *mausoleum*.

And then Grams died.

She went naturally, thank goodness. On autumn's second night, I found her in her old rocking chair, her eyes wide open. I wasn't even sad. Pa had left her. Ellerae had rotted around her. I hoped there were angels like Auntie Lessa had said, and that Grams was soaring among them.

Wherever she'd gone, it was better than our house.

I went to market six days later. No one else came. It didn't surprise me. I knew not *everyone* in the city had disappeared, but the last few survivors were probably boarded up in their houses. Not that it'd do them any good. The mayor's grandson had vanished from the top room of a seven-story tower. Guards had vanished even after locking themselves in their prisoners' cells. Husbands, wives, and children had gone missing whether wandering in open fields or sleeping in rooms barred and locked ten times over.

But no one had seen the culprit. No one had seen anything more than a shadow. Except maybe me.

With my empty basket swaying in my hand, I walked home. It was a silent walk, but I wasn't sad. I'd walled off my heart to almost everything. *Everything my memory of Gio.* I came to the streetlamp, and although the midday sun smoldered behind the clouds, the lamp burned. *White as an angel's teats,* Pa would've said. *Hot as the steam from a fresh pot of noodles.*

On the cobblestones beneath it, I saw a coin.

And then another.

And still another.

Not an accident, I knew. So I followed the trail.

The coins were for me, I guessed. I didn't know who put them there, or why, and I didn't care. If some horror snatched me up as I chased the silver line, I figured I'd lived long enough. I'd outlasted most of Ellerae, after all. Whatever happened now didn't matter.

I walked and walked and walked. The coins led me to Osso's end, then down a half dozen more alleys. I came to the grass at city's edge. It was browning already. The wind ripped across the fields, cold and biting. The sun didn't much savor autumn's arrival, and so it skulked behind walls of grey clouds, never once peeking out at me.

The trail of coins continued.

Every six steps, I found one in the grass. For a while I plunked them in my basket, but after a few hundred I gave it up and dropped the basket altogether. *Too heavy anyway*, I thought. *What good are coins if no one's left to take them?*

A ghost in a girl's shoes, I crossed the meadow between Ellerae and Lake Po. At lake's edge, the coins curled westward along the shore. I followed. Around rocks, across beaches, and through thickets they led me. There must've been thousands; the wealth of an entire city. On some of the silvers I saw Ellerae's mayor, smiling and stupid. But others were tarnished and older. Those coins looked tired and salted, as though the sea had swallowed them and spat them out. *From Tessera*, I guessed. *Pa's coins.*

Is Pa still alive?

When the coins snaked their way into the swamps west of Lake Po, I worried the trail would end. But no, it didn't. Someone had taken the time to hammer them to the trees. I'd walk six steps through the shallow, swampy broth, and I'd find another piece of silver, staked through its heart with a six-penny nail.

If Grams could've seen me then, she'd have killed me. I waded, waist-deep, into the mucky water. I saw snakes dangling from branches. I glimpsed buzzards sitting high in the trees, waiting for me to die. If I'd have made the same trek a month ago, the mosquitoes would've eaten me alive, but even now at autumn's beginning, they made a fine feast of me.

And then, wet and shivering, I crawled out of the muck and onto a rotten little island. My shoeless feet squelched in the mud. Vines as thick as Pa's forearms hung from trees taller than any tower in Ellerae. The coins stopped. I looked around, swatted another mosquito, and sagged. I was somewhere in the swamp's middle. I was lost.

Now where?

Was this a sick joke?

Is this what everyone does before they go missing?

I knew then I'd walked for longer than I'd imagined. The sun had sunk to the horizon, and the sky looked a sickly shade of purple and grey. In the deep shadows beneath the trees, I squinted.

Is that a light?

Inside one of the trees?
No. Can't be.

I walked toward the hugest tree on the swamp-island. It was bigger than my house on Osso, this tree, though it looked ready to die. On its black-barked flank, I glimpsed a gaping hole. And coming out of the hole, I saw a pallid light. I don't know why, but the tree and the light made me want to vomit. The whole place stank, but not of death. It smelled of evil.

Can't sleep here.
Didn't bring any food.
I think I may have just killed myself.
Oh well. Might as well go find what's making the light.

I walked toward the light. It reminded me of something Grams had once said about people seeing bright lights before they die. If it were true, I hoped she hadn't seen it. *Not if it looked anything like this.*

I took a deep breath and slipped inside the tree. I still didn't see the light's source, but I saw everything else well enough. The tree's guts looked like the inside of a twisted house. Tapestries hung from stakes high above. Plush red carpets tickled the bottoms of my filthy feet. White tables and chairs stood in the middle of a grand room. A curling stairway wound its way up to places higher in the tree, and another descended through a gaping hole in the floor.

Tapestries. Carpets. Tables. Chairs.
All made of people.
One of these is Gio.

Anyone with half a brain would've run. Not me. I walked up to one of the chairs, saw a sack half-filled with Pa's old coins, and plucked one of them out.

I wasn't really scared until Pa climbed up the stairs and looked at me.

"Mia," he said, unsurprised, "You're here."

I looked at him. His clothes moldered on his skinny arms. His pale, hairless scalp looked ready to rot. If someone had asked me to describe him, I'd have said, *haunted*.

And I'd have been right.

"Pa…" I backed away and dropped the coin. "What are you doing here?"

He walked up to the table and snared a silver piece out of the sack. It looked huge in his skinny, almost skeletal fingers. "I hoped you wouldn't come," he said.

"Then…why'd you leave the trail?" I shivered.

"I had to. No other way."

"No other way to *what*?"

"To be rid of it."

"To be rid of *what*?"

"My life." He narrowed his eyes. "I'm tired of it."

I almost bolted. But when I looked out into the eve, the swamp scared me enough to keep me inside.

"Pa…" I felt a tear dribble down my cheek.

He stared at me. I fell silent.

"Mia, poor Mia," he began, "You don't know what it's like."

"To be a killer?" I hissed.

"No. Never." He looked wounded. "You think *I* did all this? No. I'm just the one who helps. Who waits. Who *knows*. It's my punishment."

"I don't understand, Pa." My tears rolled down my chin. "Please…you're scaring me."

55

He hung his head. "I know. And I'm sorry. It's unforgivable. But it was the price I agreed to. If I hadn't, I'd have died with Tessera. There'd never have been a Gio. There'd never have been a *you*."

"Pa…who…? Who took all those people? It wasn't you? Who was it, then? Or…*what* was it?"

Pa looked up and down, left and right. His eyes were slitted. He was terrified. "*It's* not here now." Pa shook his head. "*It's* gone to claim the last few. And when *it's* done, it'll be my turn."

"You knew?" I swallowed my fear for a second and became angry. "You knew all along? Ma and Da? Did you know about them? And Grams? You lied to her? And Gio? Pa, how could you?"

All the light in Pa's eyes fled. He glared at me, and I fell silent. If I'd have understood then that the evil shining in him was but a tiny fragment of what awaited me, I'd have run into the swamp and drowned myself.

But I didn't.

Coward.

"Mia," he growled, "I'm tired of this life. This bargain…it burns in me. All these coins…all this death…I'm tired of helping. But it's the price I paid. Seventy more years of life, he gave me. Else my tendons would be the soft carpet under your toes. My arms and legs would fashion yon table. My blood would stain these walls cherry."

I sank to the floor. "Who made you do this?"

He stood over me. His shadow blocked out all the light. "Not who. *It. It* that poisoned Veni. *It* that slaughtered Tessera. *It* that enslaved me and made me help devour Ellerae. See those tables? That's the mayor and his children. Feel the floor beneath your knees? That's the hair of fifty maidens. The house they found...the one full of art...that's from three cities *before* Tessera. And all the while he...*it*...has been walking among us.

"And ever since Tessera, I've been helping him hide."

I couldn't talk anymore. I just knelt and quaked and swallowed my horror.

"And now it's the end." He shambled away from me. "Ellerae's gone. But there're more cities. More to the north. And farther east. More there, too. But I'm too tired. I won't let *it* have me another hour. *It* wants more of me, but *it* won't get what *it* wants. Old man, old ghoul. My bargain is up. My pain is over."

What happens now? I wanted to ask. *You're going to kill yourself? You're going to kill me?*

He came to me. He took my hand, peeled my fingers open, and stared at my sweating palm. I didn't understand the significance of his hesitation until later. Much later.

"Take this, Mia." He held out a black coin. "Take this blackened gold and make it yours."

I shivered and shook my head.

"Take it!" he demanded.

"No." My voice was a whisper. "I don't want your bargain. I don't want to work for *it*. Just kill me."

"Foolish girl!" he roared. "This coin isn't *its'* bargain. You rejected that when you rejected my coins."

You bastard, I thought. *You tried to trick me!*

57

"Do you want to live, Mia?" He pumped his jaws angrily. "You have to decide, and you have to do it now. *It's* coming back soon. *It's* going to make me into a statue or a bucket of paint or a new tapestry. You've rejected *its* bargain, and so *it'll* do the same to you. You can't run. You can't hide. You either take this coin and leave in peace. Or you stay here and be made into *pieces.*"

I almost screamed, *'Just kill me!'* But with Pa standing over me, already half dead, I wasn't so sure. "What's so special…" I quivered, "about the black coin?"

"It's the first," said Pa. "*Its'* first. You take it, and *it'll* have no power over you. Not now or ever. But if you dither a moment more, our skins'll both be stretched tonight. And it'll hurt, Mia. Oh…it'll hurt."

Coward.

I snatched the coin away and sprinted out of the tree.

As I fled, I knew Pa had told at least one final lie. *It* had been in the tree the whole time. I knew when I heard Pa's screams, when the sounds of his bones popping broke the night, and when a cloud of buzzards fled the treetops in horror of the *horror.*

Sheer willpower led me back to Ellerae. Sloppy with sweat and mud, my skin torn by tree limbs and puckered with bug bites, I staggered onto Osso and collapsed beneath the streetlamp. I didn't dream. I didn't freeze. I just slept, dead to the world, until dawn.

When I woke, the streetlamp's flame was out. I stood up and shook most of the fear out of my little bones. I wasn't cold, though I expected to be. I wasn't even hungry, even though I'd not eaten in almost a day. Ellerae was silent. I wandered around for a short while, calling out the names of the few I knew had been alive last week. But no one answered. I knew in my heart they'd either fled, killed themselves, or been made into tables and chairs.

Ellerae had died.

And no matter what Pa had promised, I'd died, too.

* * *

And so here I sit, alone in my new house. I'm still a little girl inside, but not really. The memories of Grams and Gio cling like cobwebs to my mind, too fragile to touch without destroying. I'm not in Ellerae anymore. No one is. When soldiers from the city of Milian found it, they burned it to the ground. I think they knew what had happened. They were wiser than we'd been. They cursed the 'Old Man' and chased his rumor to the west, though I doubt they ever found him. The ghoul of Tessera, Ellerae, and a hundred cities before will keep killing, keep making his precious art until everyone in the world is sticks and bones.

I suppose, had the soldiers been ever smarter, they'd have come east.

They'd have come to me, to Valai.

It's a pretty city, it is, and thrice as huge as Ellerae.

I like it in Valai. I live in a mansion at the city's edge, near a great, dark forest. I have vast empty rooms, a bottomless basement, and towers tall and sharp. I even have a streetlamp. It grows a little brighter every week.

I didn't use Pa's or Ellerae's coins to buy it.

I borrowed from the locals.

It's a fresh new evening. As I sit on my rocking chair, sewing something beautiful, I wait for the sun to set. Someone knocks on my door. I know who it is. It's the young man who's always nosing about my courtyard. He's an orphan, like so many children in Valai. I feel bad for him, if that's possible. Before I answer the door, I put down my needles and pick up a silver coin from the floor. It hurts to bend over, but I manage. My bones just aren't as supple as they used to be. Every little movement causes me pain.

I've gotten used to it.

"Hello, young man," I open the door.

He looks surprised to see me. It makes sense, considering I've always ignored his knocks until now.

"Evening, M'lady Mia," he says shyly. "You know who I am?"

"I do," I tell him.

"Then you know I've got no money, no food, no place to live. My uncle…he says I should find work. So I've been thinking…*well*…might be you need my help. You've lived here well on a hundred years. I could go to market for you. I could carry things. You've got all this space. Might be…*maybe*…you'd let me have a room to be your servant."

"You say you don't have any money?" I swing the door open and let him peer inside. He looks nervous, but only a little.

"No, ma'am. Not since mom and my brothers turned up missing last winter.

I set my crabbed fingers on his shoulder and guide him across the threshold and into the stale, musty room beyond. His skin is warm. His bones are strong. It's hard to control myself, but I do.

"Come inside, young man. There's silver aplenty if you're willing to do the right kind of work."

He walks inside, the foolish thing.

I wonder how strong he'll be once he's screaming.

I suppose I'll have to wait to find out. His timing is right. I need him for now. I'm tired girl anymore. I need a helper. Another set of eyes. Someone willing to take a few coins to help me hide things.

I offer him the coin.

He takes it with a smile.

I stretch my fingers. The little bones groan and pop. But this time it feels good.

"So it's a deal?" he asks.

"Until the end." I give him a grandmotherly look.

And I shut the door, locking him in with me.

He's mine now. He's hooked. He's like Pa had once been: alone, hungry, and desperate.

Just the kind of slave I need.

Because that's what I've become. I'm *it*. At night when I take my skin off, I'm the most horrifying thing this world has ever known. My fingers are scythes, my heart a pumping horror, and my sockets hollow as two empty graves. I don't make paintings, tapestries, or sculptures. I sew dolls, and I sell them right back to the people whose families I've dissected.

The black coin was a trick after all.

I guess I should be angry at Pa for giving it to me.

I should be, but I'm not. Because Pa's bones are a pretty work of art lying in some dark, terrible place. And me…I'll never die.

In cursing me to become a second *it*, Pa gave me a chance at vengeance. I'll take it. I'll relish it. I'll love it until the end of everything. I swear I'll kill the whole world if I have to. I'll make a tomb of Valai and every other city within a thousand leagues. I don't care how long it takes. I'll make enough dolls to fill the ocean. I'll get noticed. When Pa's master, *it*, finally comes to see what I've done and how I've done it better, I'll slaughter the old ghoul. I'll make a blanket of his skin to sleep beneath during the day. I'll turn his bones into powder and blow him off the cliffs of Tessera.

Because I owe him.

For stealing my childhood.

For making a tomb of Ellerae.

But mostly, for stealing my little brother, Gio.

"Come closer," I say to the young man. "For your help, I've got all the coins you'll ever need. I'll only need one thing from you."

"What's that?" His smile is so big it hurts to look at.

"*Everything*," I tell him.

The Skeleton Sculptor

On the morning the hunt began, we'd had a hundred men.

After three months, we were down to eleven.

We all knew how it would end.

But only a few got to see it.

My name is Costas. Those who knew me would've said I listened more than I talked. They'd have been right, of course. I was always a watcher more than a doer. I'd grown up in the Master's service, in a mountain city graven of pale stone. In the Master's Citadel, we had towers taller than anywhere else in the known world. We had women more beautiful than the sun, moon, and stars. *Why talk*, I thought, *when surrounded by such glory?*

And so I watched. And listened. And learned.

It was a perfect place, my home. I loved it.

And if I weren't dead, I'd return there and never leave again.

* * *

Most of what I remember of our ninetieth night out was that my feet hurt. I sat beneath the full red moon, the campfire snapping at my toes, and I rubbed my soles until my fingers went numb.

For a short while, I didn't care about all the men who'd gone missing.

I didn't care about the Master's orders.

All that mattered was that my sandals were off, my armor was loose on my shoulders, and my belly was full of stew. After all, there weren't many of us left to eat the food we'd started with. There seemed no sense in dying hungry.

"It's ten days home," a soldier murmured across the dying campfire. "Which means if we leave tomorrow, one of us will survive."

I looked at the other men. Five of us were hunkered in the scrub. We were sulking by the fire, our gazes inky in the night. The other six were asleep in two tents atop a nearby hill. I could see the lights of their fires dying the same as ours. The flames were red, just like the moon.

There was no wind that night. Only the scarlet light on the silent earth.

"So," Aios grumped on the fire's far side, "the one who makes it back home…he gets to die on the Master's gallows 'stead of out here in the grass."

I listened while the argument began.

"We don't *know* the others are dead," Nikolas grunted. "Could be they're hiding. Could be they're lost in the hills somewhere."

Nikolas wasn't wrong, not exactly. We'd never actually found any of the bodies. But Aios knew better. So did I. Not that I said anything.

"As likely missing as swimming on the moon." Aios glanced skyward. "They're all dead and you know it."

64

Philok, biggest of our cadre, rolled his massive shoulders. Tanned to gold by the sun, still packed into his hard leather hauberk, he was the only one of us who still looked fierce.

If any of us survive, I thought, *it'll be him.*

"I want it to come," Philok rumbled. "Let it skulk out of the darkness. I've a spear for it. There'll be no more of our bones. Only *its*."

It was wishful thinking, and we all knew it. Aios shook his head. Nikolas just looked afraid. Leuk peered over the fire, moonlight in his eyes, and went back to eating from his wooden bowl. He never talked, our Leuk. He was even quieter than me.

"Spears don't kill *ghosts*," murmured Aios.

"Mine might." Philok glared.

Our huge friend had a point. His spear, a man and a half tall, leaned on a boulder near the fire. Its haft was as thick as most men's forearms, its tip catching the moonlight just so. I'd seen Phi skewer a boar with it once. It'd split the poor, squealing thing in two.

But our quarry wasn't a boar. It didn't squeal. It didn't die.

All it did was take the living away. And never bring them back.

The men argued more. They'd done the same every night for weeks. But by now no one bothered to get truly angry. We all figured if we started killing each other, it'd only make our quarry's work easier.

Easy enough for the Ghoul already, I thought.

I rubbed my feet one last time and went to sleep.

* * *

It had started ages ago, this problem of ours.

It'd begun before I'd been born. Before the Master's great-grandfather had been born.

Before any of us.

Back then, before the Citadel, before all the pale stone cities had sprung up along the coast, it had been a better world. At least, that's the yarn our elders spun around the hearths at night. And so that's the tale we believed.

'*A fine, quiet realm*,' they used to say. '*Green pastures, hillocks teeming with olive trees, golden sun shining on endless vineyards.*'

'*And no Ghoul.*'

I'd never cared about the stories. Not as a boy, anyhow. In the Citadel, home of the Master, there'd never been any ghosts. The clap of hard sandals on marble streets had been our music, not the howls of mothers who'd lost their sons or or husbands whose wives had never come home. The stories we cared about had been of wars fought and won, of islands conquered, and of white-sand shores. We dreamed of golden coins in our pockets and raven beauties that would one day be ours if we served with honor in the Master's guard.

We'd known nothing about the Ghoul.

And our lives had been better for it.

* * *

In the morning we woke to shouts again.

"It's Saulos!" I heard Nikolas scream. "How? He slept in his armor! He's gone, but his breastplate's still here!"

"Where were you?" one of the hill-camp soldiers cursed another. "You were on watch! You were supposed to be guarding us!"

"I *was* on guard! I—"

Amid their shouts, I clawed away sleep's last cobwebs and sat up beneath the dawning sun. It was hot already, and I was tired despite having slept so well. To defend against the Ghoul's nightly visits, the others had taken to sleeping for only an hour or two at a time, if at all. Not me. I couldn't do it. I didn't want to be awake when death came for me, and so I'd almost always slept full nights…and weathered my nightmares alone.

I shambled up the hill. My sword pattered against my outer thigh, and the straps of my armor dangled without care. A year ago, I'd been a fresh recruit in the Master's service, a newly-minted member of his honored guard.

And now what am I?

Dead.

I came to Saulos' empty tent. It was just as the others had shouted. There lay his armor, all red leather and polished steel. Saulos had been a captain. His armor was better than ours, or at least prettier. It didn't much matter. It lay on the ground, almost untouched. It looked like someone had snipped the straps off and carried him away while he was sleeping. There wasn't even any blood.

As I stood there, the others fell into their ritual panic. Some muttered prayers. Others shouted that we should return to the Citadel at once. Both cries were familiar. Neither really mattered.

"*One* of us alive is better than nothing!" cried a soldier whose name I hadn't bothered to learn.

"The hell it is!" argued Aios. "You think the Master will understand when one man marches up and explains ninety-nine of his brothers are dead? He'll smile, name the survivor a deserter, and hang his body over the cliffs for the gulls to laugh at."

Aios was right. If there was one truly hard thing about life in the Citadel, it was the Master's law. He didn't suffer failure, not from his fabled soldiers. If our hundred never came home, it wouldn't matter. He'd have a feast, sacrifice a few bulls, and send out two-hundred more men.

Though somehow I knew the result would be the same.

The men argued. It got vicious. Someone cursed the Master's name. Someone else shoved Nikolas in the dirt. Philok shook his spear, and everyone finally fell silent.

I don't know why I stopped watching and started talking.

Might've ended better had I not.

"There's one place we haven't looked," I chimed in.

"Where? What place?" grunted Philok.

"The lighthouse. It's only a day south."

"Why there?" spat Aios. "It's just one cripple in a rotten tower. He's probably a hundred days dead. Besides, the lighthouse doesn't work. Doesn't need to. Ships don't use that route anymore. They come up the river."

"He's right." Nikolas stood and dusted off his armor. "We're trying to help the villagers, not some lonely old cod stuck in a tower."

They were right, of course. We'd not help anyone by marching down to the sea and visiting one old man in his tower. The lighthouse keeper didn't even have a family. Never had, not that we knew of. Even if he was still alive, we'd not do the countryside any favors by rescuing him.

But that wasn't my point. Maybe it should've been, but it wasn't.

"Nikolas, you still have the map?" I blurted.

"Aye," he said.

"Well. Fetch it."

He did. In moments he marched down the hill and back up. The others stared at me like I'd just slapped the sun out of the sky. Wouldn't have been the worst thing, considering how hot it was.

Nikolas brought me the map. It was big, the Master's chart, and I unfurled it on the hillside while several others knelt beside me.

"There." I pointed to a village by the sea. Veni, jewel of the south, sat on a beautiful beach right in the map's center. It was a new city, paid for by the Master's coin. We'd been there a month prior. None of us had wanted to leave. Until the villagers had made us.

"So it's Veni. What about it?" said Aios.

I dragged my finger eastward along the map. I stopped at a nameless black ink-blot. It was the lighthouse. I tapped it twice.

"We've been to every other village, tower, and crumbling old fort along the sea. But not the lighthouse. Not there."

No one could disagree with that. We'd marched to dozens of hamlets, fisherman's wharves, and sad little huts along the coast. All of them had lost people over the years. By the dates they'd given us, we'd figured it out. One person had gone missing every night. Just one, never more, never fewer.

For hundreds of years.

And we'd only just now worked up the courage to try to stop it.

"The lighthouse," I said, "it's right in the middle of it all."

I traced a circle with my finger. All the places that had lost people, *all of them*, lay within it. And in the circle's center sat the lighthouse.

The men stared for several moments. I figured Aios would be the first to argue. He was, after all, the smartest of us. If anyone ever forgot it, he was always sure to remind them.

"Now just you wait." Aios didn't disappoint. "The Master knew about the lighthouse. He sent men last year to scour the old tower up and down. They didn't find a thing."

"Aye," agreed Philok. "I remember. That's what started this whole mess. While our soldiers were in the lighthouse, people were disappearing in cities three and four days away. That's when the Master decided to start the hunt."

I closed my eyes. I knew what I wanted to say, just not how to say it.

"What if the Ghoul doesn't come home every night?" I finally exhaled.

"So it goes out on rounds?" Aios let out a morbid laugh.

"Maybe so," I countered. "But it still has to have a lair, right? A place to retreat? What if it's the lighthouse?"

"Nice theory, but after all these years the lighthouse would be stuffed with bones a thousand men high," said Aios. "The Master's men would've noticed, I think."

"Or they'd have found the bodies along the way," murmured Nikolas.

And they've never found any of the missing, I thought.

They're right. I'm stupid to bring it up.

But wait. There was something else I wanted to say.

Maybe it'd been a dream. Maybe something else. If the morning hadn't been so damnably hot, chances are my brain wouldn't have cooked and I'd have never remembered it.

What was it I'd thought of?

Was it a nightmare I'd had?

A memory of my childhood?

"I think I was born out here," I said.

"What?" Aios made a face.

Several of the other soldiers stood and left. I knew what they thought. They thought I was a fool wasting their time. I didn't blame them. I heard them talk about fleeing home to the Citadel. They didn't want anything to do with the map or hunting the Ghoul. They wanted to be home in their beds.

But Aios, Philok, Leuk, and Nikolas remained.

"I was born out here," I continued. "Not in Veni. But close. It was near the sea. I remember my mother. I think I do, anyway. And I remember the rocks. And the lighthouse."

"No you don't," spat Aios. "You were born in the Citadel, same as us. It's just another of your dreams."

"What if—" I started.

"I wasn't born in the Citadel either." Philok came to my rescue. "I'm from the mountains. My father was dying, so they brought me down to the Master's fortress. My family figured I'd never have a life unless I served in the guard."

Aios looked stunned. I nodded at Philok, grateful.

"I remember walking on the shore." I stared off into the sky. "My mother sent me off to play while she worked. At least, I think she did. One day, I wandered near the lighthouse. I remember it. It was above me. *Way* above. And I remember seeing something in the cliffs beneath it. Was it holes? Breaks? Cracks in the rock?"

"Holes?" Aios shook his head.

"I think he means caves," said Nikolas.

I looked at the three of them. They'd been my brothers for the last year. They knew I didn't talk much, but when I did, I meant what I said.

"That's right." My eyes were wide. "Caves."

It hadn't been a dream.

I'd just remembered a part of my childhood.

And my mother, who'd I been made to forget.

* * *

Clouds gathered over the sea. Greys and blues smoldered in the sky, darker than the water. The hour was only late afternoon, yet the world looked ready for twilight.

We were terrified.

We'd every right to be.

The five of us mounted a last hill and caught sight of the distant lighthouse. It was an old, old thing, its stones bleached skeleton-white. It'd been built long before the Master's time, long before any of us. I couldn't help but wonder how many of the Ghoul's prey the lighthouse had watched vanish.

One every night.

Hundreds of years.

I couldn't make the numbers work in my head.

We'd walked all day. Ever since we'd split up from the other soldiers, I hadn't said a thing. Phi, Aios, Nikolas, and Leuk had decided to join me. The others had chosen to go back to the Citadel and face the Master's wrath.

Our group hadn't lost anyone last night.

And so we all knew what had happened.

"I hope it took Diok," chuffed Aios as we walked down the hill and into the fields between us and the lighthouse. "Never liked that prick."

Nikolas sighed, "Maybe it'll follow *them* instead of *us*. That'll give us what...three more days?"

"Maybe." Philok's knuckles were white around his spear. "But what if there's more than one Ghoul?"

None of us had ever thought of that before.

We shivered the notion away and kept walking.

73

The five of us drew nearer the lighthouse. Switches of dry grass skirled at our waists, dancing wildly in the wind. My feet hurt again. My ankles, too. The grass had nicked me in a hundred little places. If the Ghoul didn't kill me, I half-believed the fields might drown me.

At least it's not hot anymore.

By the time we came to the cliff, upon which the lighthouse stood tall and formidable, the rain began. The wind hit us and the storm's droplets beaded on our sunburned skin. I looked my companions over. To a man, we savored standing in the rain. It was an island of peace in a world of despair.

"Are we going in?" Nikolas nodded.

"The lighthouse?" Aios smirked. "Why should we? We know what's in there. Nothing."

"Might be wise to weather the storm in there," Philok held his huge palm open to catch the rain.

Aios looked annoyed. But then again, he always did.

"Fine."

I knocked at the lighthouse door. The oak plank must've been two-hundred years old. It felt soft as soap beneath my knuckles. I rapped it ten times before Philok pushed me aside and kicked the thing in. I'd hoped the old man would answer. But the moment Nikolas fired a torch and walked into the great round room beyond the door, we knew the lighthouse had gone untended for months.

"Think he died all alone in here? Somewhere up there near the top?" Aios's voice echoed in the void.

"Maybe the Ghoul got him," said Philok.

"Why would it bother?" Aios cracked. "Old man was damn near a hundred. Pointless to kill what's already dead."

Except the Ghoul doesn't care, I almost said. *He takes children. Pregnant women. Venerable old men. And soldiers.*

We used pieces of the broken door to light a fire. With it blazing, we peeled off our armor and hunkered down in the shadows. The rain shattered the world beyond the lighthouse walls, harder than anything I'd ever heard. It didn't feel natural. Bitter breezes flew into the windows, and stray drops of water swirled into the room, stinging our shoulders. No matter where I sat, the rain found me. I finally settled on the spot farthest from the fire. Leuk, stoic and silent, shook his wet hair when he sat down beside me.

"Maybe you were right." Aios smirked at me while cooking up a pot of stew. "This place is creepy. I hate it. That old man's body is probably up those stairs. The Ghoul's probably waitin' for us."

"How do you suppose we kill it? I mean really, *really* kill it," asked Nikolas.

"The Ghoul?" Philok rubbed his forehead.

"No, the fucking rain," quipped Aios. "Of course he means the Ghoul."

Philok didn't flinch. "This spear." He flicked the blade of his man-and-a-half tall weapon. "Or Costas' sword. Or Leuk's daggers. Doesn't matter. Everything dies."

"Does it?" Nikolas looked afraid again. "It's been a few hundred years, right? It should've been dead by now. What if it *can't* die? What if it's…forever?"

Philok thought about it for a moment, and then huffed. "There's probably no such thing as the Ghoul. It's probably a family of murderers. Might be they've passed down the family secret over the generations. Fathers teaching sons…*hell*…mothers teaching daughters. 'Here's how best to kill a man, lassie,' they tell the little ones. 'A drug in his wine to make him sleep, then a knife between his ribs. No one'll be the wiser. Not even the Master.'"

No one laughed except Aios.

I might've known.

We set up a watch. I went first, else I'd never have woken for second shift. The rain raged as I tightened my armor and laid my sword atop my thighs. I probably should've been afraid. As it turned out, I'd little energy left for fear.

I didn't remember falling asleep that eve. I suffered no dreams, no nightmares. One moment I was sitting beside the fire, the mist collecting on my shoulders.

And when I woke, Nikolas was gone.

The others were still dozing. It'd been Aios's turn to watch, but he was curled up beside the long-dead fire, looking little different than a sleeping boy. Dawn's first glow crept into the high windows. In a pool of soft light lay Nikolas's armor, his blanket, and his bowl.

And his sword, still in its scabbard.

If I shout, it'll go like it always does, I thought. *I'll be quiet.*

I knelt beside the patch of stone Nikolas had slept on. He'd lain there for some time, it appeared. The mist had gathered all around him, but his blanket was dry. I touched the brittle fabric, and in the cold light examined it.

No blood.

Not torn.

Almost like he left willingly.

And then there was his armor. The straps were sliced clean through, the same as scissors through twine. Looking at the hunk of leather and steel, I wasn't sure why we even bothered with armor anymore. The Ghoul wasn't afraid of it.

The Ghoul wasn't afraid of anything.

I looked at my hand. My knuckles were bloodless. I realized I was squeezing my sword.

For all the good our weapons do.

I woke Philok first. He came to with a jolt, seizing my throat in his massive hand.

"Phi—" I coughed.

He let go of me. As I knelt there gasping, something in my eyes gave the truth away.

"Who's gone?" he rumbled.

"Niko." I sagged.

"No blood? No one heard him?"

"Nothing." I rubbed my neck. "It's morning now. He's only been missing for a little while."

We woke the others. For once, there was no panic. Leuk said nothing. He looked stoic as ever, no different than if he'd slept in his bunk at the Citadel. Frowning, Aios kicked at Nikolas's things and glared at the rest of us, but kept his curses beneath his breath. This was what it had come to. We were dying one by one, and we hardly even minded anymore.

After a time, Philok dropped a helmet on his head, shouldered his spear, and marched to the bottom of the stairs that led to the lighthouse's top. The weathered stone stairwell twisted up through a gaping hole in the ceiling. No sunlight spilled down from above. The inky darkness of the lighthouse's hollow heart oozed down onto Philok's face.

"I'm going up there," he grunted.

I expected an argument. But Aios plucked up Niko's sword, unsheathed his own, and nodded at Philok with both blades in hand. "I'm coming with you," he said.

Leuk and I had no other choice.

With Philok in front and Leuk in the rear, the four of us stalked up the stairs. We emerged into the void above the room we'd slept in, and we saw slender shafts of light carving pallid lines into the darkness. The windows on the lighthouse's sides were shuttered. The climb to the tower top would be done mostly in shadow.

Step by step, we marched. The lighthouse felt a thousand steps high. The musty air filled our lungs, while plumes of dust from our footfalls floated the same as stars at midnight. We wound our way up through the cold emptiness, at last arriving at the door to the lighthouse's top. None of us knew what to expect. I held my sword with no more confidence than when I'd first set foot in the Master's training garden.

"If anything's on the other side," Phi whispered, "kill it. Don't stop cutting until your blades are down to nubs."

We all nodded. Aios cracked a wicked smirk. Philok shouldered the door with all his might, breaking the door to pieces.

The sunlight poured over us.

We invaded the lighthouse's top room. We were an army, the four of us, a cloud of fear and steel. Philok roared when he went in, and Aios growled. Leuk and I didn't make a sound, but we were ready. Our blades were as sharp as any in the world. And they should've been, for we'd never used them.

But there was nothing in the room.

No caretaker.

No bodies.

No sea of bones or carpet of skin.

Philok looked disappointed. Halting in the sunlight, he rapped the butt of his spear on the floor and glared at everything. As for me, I couldn't help but be relieved. I let my sword sag and my shoulders droop. After all, the sunlight in the tower's top was warm and soothing. It swam over me, gliding in from each of thirty windows, sparkling on the giant glass lens in the room's center.

I figured it was the last time I'd ever feel warm.

No. I didn't figure. I *knew*.

"It wasn't ever up here," cursed Aios. "We're idiots."

"We still had to check," argued Philok.

"Yes…well." Aios shook his head. "We checked. And nothing. So now what?"

"Costas's caves," said Philok.

I could tell Aios had expected Phi to say it. "No. Not yet," he grumbled. "Breakfast first."

Too soon, we abandoned the warmth of the lighthouse's top. I felt sad to leave so quickly. Halfway down into the dark, I realized I'd never even taken the chance to look out across the sea.

At the bottom, Aios prepared breakfast for us. It was hard tack and fried cakes softened with hot water, same as most mornings. It didn't much matter. Cooking had always calmed Aios, so we never complained.

With only a rotten beam of lighthouse timber to burn, Aios' kindling of choice that morn was Nikolas's satchel. Nikolas didn't need it, after all. But just as Aios snared the leather bag and began cutting it to shreds with his knife, I stopped him.

"Wait," I said, "Something's in there."

Aios made a face. "It's just a book. Tear out the pages. It'll save us from sending Leuk out to collect things to burn."

"No…" I grabbed the bag and pulled the book out. "Just use the satchel. Let me keep this. I want to see what Niko wrote."

Aios squeezed his eyes shut. He looked like he wanted to kill me. "Fine," he muttered. "But remember; the dead can't read."

While Aios cooked and Philok rummaged through the rest of Niko's things, I sat in a pool of sunlight and cracked the book open. It was well-made, a far finer thing than Nikolas had any right to possess. I couldn't believe that with all my hours of watching, I'd never seen him with it. And then, when

Philok grunted that he'd found a quill and a vial of ink, it hit me. I understood.

Nikolas had been keeping a journal.

The book has the Master's mark on it.

Niko had always been a lazy soldier.

But he'd learned to write far sooner than the rest of us.

The rest of the world fell away, and soon it was just me and the journal. I read dozens of entries. Nikolas had done his work well. He'd catalogued how much food we'd had, our movements beyond the Citadel, the people we'd questioned, and the names and ranks of the soldiers that had vanished. He'd even written the dates they'd gone missing.

I skimmed across as much as I could. Most of it was trivial, but the deeper I read, the more I saw of Niko's personal comments.

And the more I was filled with dread.

He'd written things like:

One soldier from Camp B gone in the night. Left his armor and sword. No blood. Same night: A man from Camp C swore he saw a shadow moving. The camps: an hour apart.

Rained hard last eve. Saulos's tent-mate was taken. Grigora says he found tracks in the mud. Not one set, but two. Not sandal prints. Bare feet.

Another gone last night. Bibi – Captain, 1st Company. But Camp D, upon returning from the city, says that Veni lost someone that same eve. It's always been one a night. But maybe this was more.

Does it mean two Ghouls?

Occurred to me that we should look beyond our borders. Ask if others have vanished on the same dates. I know we can't – they're our enemies in the North and West, but still.
More than two Ghouls?

Why is it hunting only soldiers now?

Does it know we're coming?

Will it stop?

I closed the cover. I couldn't read any more. Aios dropped a wooden bowl in my lap and snorted. "Boring read?" he chuffed. "Books are for scholars, Cos. Now give it over. We'll use it to make a fire for tonight's dinner."

"No." I pushed his hand away. "I'm going to finish it."

"Finish it?"

"Yes. Reading it. And *writing* it."

"Why? You'll be dead soon."

"I know, but—"

"Fine. Keep the damn thing. Whatever helps you die better."

I ate in silence. I say *silence* even though Aios talked the entire time. He rambled about how our lives had become meaningless, how our deaths wouldn't matter because we had no children, no lands, and no possessions beyond our weapons and armor. Maybe it was true. Maybe we were dead men no matter what we did. But when he said *meaningless*, it didn't sit right with me. Whether the Ghoul killed us for sport or the Master hung us for being failures, it seemed wrong to just let it happen.

I have to make it meaningful, I thought.

The journal. I'll finish it.

Maybe someone will find it.

After breakfast, a deep quiet overtook the four of us. There was no fleeing for the Citadel now, we knew. Unless the Ghoul abandoned his hunt, we'd all be dead within eight days. And so we sat there for a time, sharpening our swords needlessly. I like to think we dwelled on the purpose of our lives, the good things we'd seen, and all the glory we'd hoped for.

But I knew better.

Philok dreams of destroying the Ghoul. Of being heroic.

Aios dreams of how he'd have done it if he were the Master.

Leuk dreams of the life he wanted. Of what might've been had he finished his twenty years of service.

And what do I dream of?

Death.

And then it ended. Philok stood, spear in hand, and looked at us. We didn't say anything to him. We gathered our swords, strapped on our armor, and doused the fire. In a short, ragged line, we trailed Phi out into the sunlight.

And for all the glamour of the great blue sky, we felt the shadow upon us.

We left the lighthouse and walked to the cliff's edge. As the tower fell behind us, I looked over my shoulder at it. The edifice was white as death. Its sides were smooth and ashen, its outer walls seamless. The old thing looked like it had sprouted right out of the cliffs. I was glad to be rid of it. I don't know why, but I promised myself I'd write about it in Niko's journal.

"Costas." Aios' voice pulled me out my daydream. "Wake the hell up. We can't get down from here. See?"

I gazed over the cliffs and onto the dark ocean. The water boiled over the shore far below, the waves black and foaming. I imagined if one of us fell over the edge, we could've counted to ten before we hit the rocks. Aios was right. From our vantage, there was no way to reach the shore.

Or the caves.

"We'll have to go—" I began.

"To Veni," Philok grunted.

In hindsight, I should've suggested we find another way down. A quicker way.

But Veni it was.

We marched.

And marched.

And marched.

That eve, tired and sweating, we descended out of the cliffs. Veni lay before us, sprawling and fresh beneath the violet sunset. It wasn't a big city, but it was still beautiful at twilight. Strands of hanging lamps lit its rooftops the same as the stars. The waves were too rough for sailing, but I could see the masts stark against the sky, and I could hear the people's laughter. I envied them. But I knew as soon as we soldiers were gone, the Ghoul would go back to hunting at random.

Some from the countryside.
And some from Veni.

"We shouldn't go in there," I said to the others.

"Why not?" Aios stared at me.

"We're bad luck. We're hunted men. Veni knows us. Even if they don't kick us out, we'll not be welcome."

"The Master's soldiers can't be refused," Aios argued. "If they deny us, it's under pain of death."

I looked down at the dirt path leading into the city. Sandy scrub and lonely trees pocked the twilit way. The sky was cloudless; no rain threatened us. There were a thousand places we could camp if we liked.

"I just don't think we should," I said. "The city can't protect us. No one can."

Aios looked ready to split me in half. "Fine. We'll stay the night out here," he said. "In the sand. In the dirt. If the Ghoul comes, you're first."

I almost hoped so. Not because I wanted to die. But because I wanted to *know*.

Beneath the endless stars, we made our silent camp. No one from Veni noticed us. Or if they did, they didn't care. I'd rarely seen a night sky so bright as that eve. A million white pinpricks in a perfect black sheet, it seemed. Leuk and I stared at it for a long, long while.

By the dying campfire, I wrote my first words in Niko's journal:

We make for caves east of Veni. Four of us left: Costas, Philok, Leuk, and Aios.

We don't hope to find anything. We're going anyway. If nothing's there, it's my (Costas') fault. I convinced them to do this by a feeling in my gut.

And there's something else.
I think the lighthouse is made of bones.

I closed the journal. I needed to focus. We'd agreed to do a double watch: Leuk and I first, then Phi and Aios.

I worried I'd fall asleep.

But it was Aios who drifted off during his watch.

And Philok who went missing.

I woke with Aios' boot in my ribs. It hurt. I squinted into the early sunlight and saw him standing over me. He scowled, Phi's spear shaking in his grasp. *He's gone mad,* I thought. *He's going to save the Ghoul some trouble and run me through.* But he didn't. He just glowered and spat in the sand.

"Get up," he said.

I complied.

"The caves. Take us now. Let's finish this."

"But—"

"It's fine if nothing's there. I won't blame you. I might *kill* you, but I won't blame you."

We didn't eat breakfast. We didn't mourn Philok. Walking ahead of Aios and his spear, Leuk and I led the way down to the shore. At the ocean, a lone child saw us marching. He stood in the foamy shallows, throwing rocks into the water. He smiled at us, watching us long enough to see us pass into the shadow of a stark and terrible cliff. I thought it strange to see the boy all alone. He reminded me of myself, of all the mornings I must've spent doing the same as he.

We walked into the shadows. And he was gone.

"I dreamed last night," I said as I walked on the narrow strip of sand between the ocean and the cliff.

"No one cares," answered Aios.

"I heard a woman laughing." I ignored him. "She whispered something in my ear. She had dark hair. She was beautiful. I didn't want to wake up, even with you kicking me."

"A shame you'll never meet her," he mocked.

Maybe I will, I wanted to say.

We marched. Was it for many hours? Or much less? I couldn't have said. The ocean crashed against the rocks and swirled at our knees, drowning out all the world's sounds. Guarded by the mighty cliff, the sunlight never quite reached us. But the shadows and the cold couldn't slow me. I slogged on, convinced I was going to my doom, certain I still had some part to play.

This is what madness feels like, I thought. *All these years of not much talking, and now the loudest voice is in my head.*

And then we came to it, a great dark hole in the cliff wall. The ocean roared in and out of it, and the rocks like teeth crowned its top and sides. Twenty men standing side-by-side could've marched into the cavern's mouth.

And all of them would be eaten.

"Fucking lovely." Aios marched past me. He still had Phi's spear in his grasp, and he was wet up to his chest in seawater. The salt stuck to him, *and us*, in powdery white patches. We were miserable. We hadn't eaten all day.

"Got a lantern?" he spat at Leuk. Leuk shook his head.

"Torches," I murmured. "Just three."

"We've got some daylight left." Aios pointed Phi's spear into the darkness. "Let's go kill this thing. Just think...we'll be heroes."

I fired a torch, and in we went.

We were fifty steps deep when I realized what we'd gotten ourselves into. The ocean's rush faded at our backs, and the absence of light swallowed us. I squinted in the dark and saw other tunnels, black branches trailing into the underworld. I remembered a story someone had once told me about such places, and why no one should ever go into them.

"Four different tunnels." Aios saw them, too. "Wonder how deep they go."

I wished Philok had still been alive. He'd have known which tunnel to choose.

"That one's half underwater." Aios nodded at the farthest tunnel. The black hole gazed back at us, smiling as if aware of our fear.

"So we're going into this one." Aios pointed his spear at the nearest cave. It sat above us, its archway crusted in ancient limestone. A pile of broken shells sat beneath its mouth, deposited by the sea. It was the narrowest of the four.

And the darkest.

Leuk and I didn't argue. We clambered up the shells ahead of Aios. At the tunnel's mouth, I held the torch into the darkness and saw that it went down. *Way* down. Aios climbed up beside me, snared the torch from my grasp, and smirked at me as he marched straight into the blackness. "Three men wide," he laughed at us. "It's perfect. Not scared, are you?"

We were, but it didn't matter.

Down, down we went into the cave. I couldn't believe any place in the world could be so dark. The ocean's crash fell away to nothing. The only sounds were the torch's snaps and our rotten boots squelching on the stone.

We walked for what felt like an hour. Then two. The tunnel never narrowed, never widened. The air tasted stale. White powder sloughed off the walls wherever we touched, and our boots left footprints in places no other men had ever been. I was sure night had fallen outside, but I'd have given anything to be back out there, to let the Ghoul steal me from sleep instead of moldering away after a long, slow walk to the world's bottom.

Our first torch died. We lit another. Moments later, we slunk out of the tunnel and into an unthinkably vast grotto. It was truly massive, the cavern we'd found. Our torch felt like a candle in the great darkness. Far above, a lone shaft of moonlight cut through a hole in the ceiling and pooled in the grotto's center.

"What is this place?" I whispered.

"A cave. Big as Veni." Aios' gaze was wide and black. "A giant, empty coffin."

"No. Not empty," I observed.

I'd seen caves before. In the mountains east of the Citadel, we'd walked through tunnels and grottos. They'd had growths in them, daggers of lime and ancient rock. There had been beauty in those caves, elegance in the way nature had carved them.

But the shapes in this cave were different.

They were sculptures.

Something had made them.

We didn't say a word. We were too scared to talk, and too weary. Wandering out into the pool of moonlight, we gazed at the many hundreds of pale, ghostly statues standing on the grotto's floor. They were graven of white stone, and in my heart I knew they were made of the same stuff as the lighthouse.

Bones.

Human bones.

Most of the statues were of people. We glimpsed beautiful maidens holding decanters. We saw smiling children, some holding hands and standing in great rings, others all alone. As we walked through the pale, silent gallery of thousands, we saw old men and venerable ladies, soldiers and wealthy lords, beggars, fishermen, and stoic hunters. The sculptures were beautiful in a way. Whoever, or *whatever* had carved them had a talent like no other.

Somewhere in the midst of it all, Leuk tapped me on the shoulder. I looked back and saw horror in his eyes.

"What is it?" I felt myself turn pale.

He pointed at a row of sculptures removed from the rest. I took Aios' torch and forged into the dark. We came to it, the part of the cavern struck least by the moonlight, and we stood there with our mouths open.

"Monsters," I exhaled.

"Demons," we heard Aios whisper.

The sculptures in the shadows were not of men or maidens, children or village elders. They were of monsters, malevolent and skeletal, with talons in place of hands, pale knives instead of teeth, and faces made of nightmares. Some had horns. Others had tails. All of them had strange writing on their skin, words and sigils from a language none of us knew. But the true terror lay in their empty eye sockets, which were huge and full of evil.

As I stood there, breathing not at all, I believed in my heart these statues mimicked creatures that must have existed. "How else could they look so real?" I uttered without knowing it.

Aios pointed his spear at one of the horrific sculptures. He looked wild with fear, sweating and cursing beneath his breath.

"We have to destroy them," he hissed.

"How?" I argued. "There's thousands. *Tens* of thousands."

"Fine. We have to find what made them. Find it and kill it."

"What if…" I looked up at one of the horrors. "…what if *these* are what the Ghoul looks like?"

"All the more reason to kill it," Aios growled.

I didn't know where to start. My fingers went numb, and a chill crawled down my backbone. We stood there, the three of us, gazing into the grotto, stricken still with our terror.

It would've taken us hours to search the cave.

As it turned out, we didn't have to look at all.

The first thing I heard was the patter of footsteps. Aios and Leuk heard it, too. *Bare feet, I* thought. *But...small?*

Aios waved his spear in the direction of the sound. He crouched, looking deadly and afraid. And then I saw it, a little boy darting between the sculptures. He was naked, pale as a fish, and faster than any child had a right to be. At ten paces, he climbed atop a sculpture and leapt from its head to another, smiling all the way.

I shouted. Leuk pulled his daggers out.

The boy. It's him...the one throwing rocks on the beach, I thought.

We were too slow.

The boy leapt from atop the statue of a milkmaid. Aios spun, screamed, and jabbed with his spear. He missed. The boy landed on Aios's head, and Aios started screaming. I don't know what happened to me. As they struggled, I just stood there with my sword in one hand and the torch in the other. It was like I knew:

No matter what I do, we're dead.

I never expected Leuk to be the brave one. *Never.* The boy clung to Aios's head, clawing and snarling. As Aios squealed, Leuk stuck his dagger into the boy's back. For a single breath I allowed myself to hope.

Leuk's done it. I backed away. *He's saved us. No.*

Three times Leuk plunged his dagger between the boy's ribs, and three times he drew it out. If the boy felt anything, I saw no sign. No blood oozed from

Leuk's steel. The boy's skin opened up like dry, cracked parchment, but knitted itself closed within moments. I didn't understand how such a thing was possible. Nothing the Citadel's wise men had told us lived up to the truth.

With one of Leuk's daggers still in its back, the boy-Ghoul leapt off Aios' head. He looked up at us, still smiling, as Aios collapsed dead on the cavern floor. I saw no blood. I couldn't conceive how so small a creature had killed one of the Master's warriors. I was paralyzed. My sword felt as though it were made of paper. My blood felt like water in the last moments before a long winter's freeze.

The boy-Ghoul dragged Aios into the shadows. Leuk stared at me, and then went after them. I swallowed so hard it wounded my throat. I knew what was about to happen. Somehow, someway, I knew. And when I heard a second set of bare feet pattering, and when Leuk cried out his last breath, I sank to the floor in a puddle of my own fear. Perhaps it was cowardice. I knew my sword wouldn't matter.

So I didn't even try.

Many thousands of breaths went in and out of me. I closed my eyes, and the world went dark. I don't know whether I slept, but at some point I lifted my head from the floor and gazed into the darkness. The second torch had burned out, and so I fired another. It burned beside me as I sat there, a red whisper in the vast darkness.

There was but one thing left to do.

I opened Niko's journal, dipped the quill into the last of his ink, and wrote:

There is more than one Ghoul. There may be dozens. Or hundreds.

In a cave east of Veni, they hide.

They've been here for thousands of years, I believe.

They sculpt whatever they kill. Murder is their art.

They made the lighthouse.

They made the cliffs.

They took Aios and Leuk last night.

Tonight they'll come for me.

The ink was almost gone. I only had a few strokes of Niko's quill left. I don't what made me do it, but I stood and walked to the most terrifying of the Ghoul's demonic sculptures. I wasn't as afraid anymore. I stuck the torch in the creature's hand, held Niko's journal before me, and started drawing the strange symbols and words graven into the sculpture's skin. The words were old, old things. Maybe they were magic, if such a thing existed. I'd already shut the boy-Ghoul out of my mind, but for him to have survived Leuk's knives meant something I'd never understand was at work.

I drew as many of the words and symbols as I could. When the ink ran out, I hunkered down and gazed into the dark. I left the book on my lap. I had the foolish hope someone would find it one day. The shaft of moonlight was far away, not enough to see by. I knew when my torch burned out, I'd die even if the Ghouls never came for me.

I didn't have to wait long.

94

Within a hundred breaths, I heard their bare feet on the cavern's cold floor. The boy came first. He was naked and ghostly pale. White powder, surely bone dust, coated his arms up to his elbows. His fingernails were crusted in dried blood. He'd been sculpting, I was sure.

My sword lay beside me. I didn't bother to pick it up.

And then the second Ghoul came. I didn't know what I expected, but it wasn't *her*. Naked and beautiful, she walked into the yellow sphere of light made by my torch. Her hair was raven, her eyes pale blue lanterns. She wasn't terrifying at all, at least not yet.

"I dreamed of you," I said to her.

She didn't flinch.

"Are all of these your work?" I regarded the thousands of sculpted dead.

She shook her head. *Only some of them*, she told me without words.

I sat, limp and sweating, and looked at them. The boy was her ward, her student, or maybe even her child. She tousled his hair, and a plume of bone powder drifted into the torchlight.

He's the next in line, I thought.

She's teaching him.

Just like another taught her.

Without moving any other part of my body, I extended my arm and set Niko's journal into the nook between two sculptures' feet. I left my sword where it lay. It occurred to me that I'd never once used it. Ever.

The Master would've stretched my neck just for that.

The boy-Ghoul started for me, but the woman held him back.

And then she showed me what she was.

With her fingers, she pried the flesh back from her cheeks. She tore like sackcloth; the sound alone made me sick. Next she peeled back the flesh from her arms and collarbone. She was one of them, one of the monsters so perfectly sculpted behind me. Her true fingers were boney claws, her real face a horror of white bone. She had no blood in her. She was all sinew and marrow, a skeleton wrapped in human skin.

I understood why none of the missing soldiers had cried out.

She'd probably never shown them the creature beneath her skin.

All they'd seen was a beautiful woman or a handsome little boy.

And when she killed me, it didn't even hurt.

The Circle Macabre

My name is Erisa.

It's true. I'm a woman.

None of the men wanted this task.

And so it fell to me.

It'd been a long, hard road to Valai. The city was as beautiful as everyone had said it would be. Under the Queen's rule, it had prospered. Even if our rivals had thought to invade, Valai's glory would've caused their swords to rust and their fires to die. Beyond a great, dark forest it sat, in the shadow of Pala Mountain. Its towers' spires were hewn of white stones, and its streets lined with statues of heroes a thousand years gone.

And yet, for all Valai's wonder, it wasn't the city it once had been. It was quieter. It was subdued. Its people knew what was happening. But they did nothing to stop it.

It's to Valai I went to find the answers.

And it's there I intended to finish my hunt.

On the first night, I allowed myself to rest. To bathe. To sleep. After supper, the innkeep dropped seven hot stones into my bath, and I sat there in the water, soaking to my bones. I must've dozed off. Hours later, long after every lantern had been snuffed, I awoke in the cold water. I wasn't chilled. I felt as clean and relaxed as in years.

But I'd let my guard down.

And that wasn't acceptable.

The next morning I woke in the tiny, third-story room the innkeep had prepared for me. The sun hadn't quite leapt over the mountains, and starlight poked into my window. For all my need of privacy, I'd left the shutters open all night. I'd been on the road so long; I needed the open air.

In the deep, predawn quiet, I climbed out the window and hunkered on the slanted roof. Shadows swam in the alley beneath me, while the streets beyond were silent. Even without the sun, Valai was a beautiful sight. The rooftops were colored black, grey, and deep blue, not unlike the ocean on a calm morning. At ease, I lay my sword across my thighs and leaned back to watch the sun crawl into heaven.

This is it, I thought. *My last moment of peace.*

The same as I had every dawn for the last ten years, I tugged my sword from its scabbard and let the first sunlight touch the steel.

Still pretty, I thought.

Even after all the death it's seen.

Just one more, Erisa.

Just one.

My sword was three feet of blue-silver perfection. I don't know how it never lost its edge or why it never showed the slightest signs of rust. I remember thinking I should've named it. Something beautiful, I'd always wanted. But which name to choose, I couldn't ever have decided.

I suppose the sword's magic, if you could've called it that, slept in the language graven on the blade. They'd found the words in a book, tattered and

98

torn on a beach far away from everything. How the blacksmiths had known to etch the strange sigils into the steel, I'll never guess. But they'd done it. And since then my sword had been unbreakable.

And more than that, it'd been the only thing in the world capable of destroying the *Horrors*.

Because when I said my sword had seen a lot of death, I didn't mean that it had taken lives. All those years, I'd never used it on a living thing. I'd flashed it hundreds of time of course, but not to kill people. The things I had destroyed weren't really alive. They were something else, something worse. By the time I'd come to Valai, I'd consumed twenty years of my life hunting them. I'd killed hundreds of the creatures, I think. I'd lost count long ago.

As I sat on the inn's roof, I was thirty-six years old. My youth was gone. I was practically a hag.

Quite a life.

How did I choose this?

I can't remember.

I slid back into the window, dressed in my plain grey tunic, and tethered my sandals to my feet. I caught a glimpse of myself in a cracked mirror the innkeep had left on the table. I was still pretty, I suppose. I'd had a child years ago. It had been an accident, and I'd slowed my hunt to try to raise the little boy. Turns out I hadn't been much of a mother. Love wasn't a part of my soul. After four short years, I'd left him in the care of others.

Because I was driven by something else.

To be a hunter.

But never knowing why.

That morning, as the sun warmed Valai's stones, I walked through the city. It felt strange to be in the presence of so many others. Women streamed to the markets, men to the fields, while children sprinted up and down the streets. It almost looked normal. But every time I strode by a statue, every doll I saw in every child's hands, I felt the tension pluck my bones.

Might take two-hundred years.

Might take a thousand.

But this city will go empty like all the rest.

Of all the cities I'd been to, Valai was by far the biggest. I walked streets two-thousand steps long. I passed bazaars teeming with tents and merchants. Pale towers watched over me, some empty, others filled with nobles. No one paid me much attention. I must've looked like a vagabond. I was dressed in drab colors, my hair short and plain, my scabbard swaying down to my knees.

The people didn't notice me.

But I noticed them.

For no matter Valai's size, no matter that it had enough people to replace almost all those who'd gone missing, I saw what I expected to see.

Empty houses.

Merchant stalls abandoned.

Lonely, lost mothers and fathers, wandering the alleys like ghosts.

Children hunkered in the shadows.

I walked through midday. Beyond the city walls, the clouds crept over the forest and marched against Pala Mountain. I hadn't hardly noticed the chill in the air until I traded a copper coin for an apple and chomped into it. The red fruit was cold against my teeth. It hurt a little.

A storm was coming.

No doubt caused by the Horror.

In a city this vast, I knew finding the creature would not be easy. It could've lurked in Valai's sewers, sleeping in the muck by day and butchering by night. It might've holed up in any of the towers, watching its prey go about their lives. I knew it couldn't be any of the people on the streets. But by nightfall, any one of them could've been gone.

And in the morning a new statue will stand.

Or a child will happen upon a new doll.

And somehow they'll keep going about their lives.

The sky wept. A cold rain washed over me. Most people scurried inside. Alone, I kept walking. I'd traveled so many years and slept so many nights beneath the clouds that no weather bothered me anymore. The water made lines on my face and darkened my tunic. I ran my fingers through my hair, making wet spikes of my stiff, raven locks.

I probably looked like I'd lost my mind.

But I'd never felt sharper in my life.

The rain had that effect on me.

That first day, for all my walking, I found nothing I hadn't expected. I knew how this game would be played. In a city this big, I'd have to be patient. Which, so close to the end, would be hard.

* * *

That evening, I wandered all the way to Valai's grandest tavern. They'd named it Piraeus, after the man who'd built it a hundred years ago. Thoroughly soaked, I strode up its broken stone stairs, slid through an ancient oak door, and walked into a room as smoky and dark as any I'd ever inhabited. Here, the people noticed me. From a warren of tables and chairs, I caught smiles, stares, and grimaces directed my way. I imagined they didn't care for a woman with a sword marching through the doors of their city's most hallowed inn.

But I cared even less than they.

That night, and for seven after, I sat in Piraeus' Inn.

Some eves I found alcoves, and others I lurked at tables out in the open. The first night, a man tried to sit with me. I said nothing to him, and every eve thereafter no one bothered me. Always the place was filled with the noise of drunken, raucous people. Their clamor made picking out single conversations hard, but their drunkenness made finding answers easy.

And the longer I listened, the more I heard:

"We've not had good bread since Cael went gone."

"I miss Anna. All the boys on Cuther Row do. She was a real pearl, she was. And then, pluck! She stopped working her corner. Vanished, her the same as the other'uns."

"When's the last time we had good fish? Been years, right? No one delivers anymore. They know once they come here, there's no leavin'. Not without dyin', leastways."

This and much more the people offered. They were so casual about it. They knew that on any given night, odds were they and theirs would survive to see the sun rise again. But there was a weariness about them. Men groaned they'd never see another city in their lives. Women shook their heads with sadness, longing for husbands that had tried to flee years prior. It wasn't sadness I sensed in them. It was *resignation*.

Such was the Horror's way. It took one a night, every night, unless a large group of people tried to escape. In those cases the entire group went missing. A few dozen sometimes, and other times hundreds. Gone forever. Just like that.

I say gone.

I mean *dead*.

On my eighth night at Piraeus' Inn, with the smoke swirling and the tabletops damp with ale, I sat in a corner booth. I'd traded forty coppers for a city map that day, and I had it spread before me. My table looked like the oldest plank of oak in the world. The dark, stained wood had deep lines in it. A thousand drinks had been spilled on it, I sensed, and ten times as many elbows planted atop it.

From the forest around Valai, I reckoned.

From before the Horror came here.

By then, the Piraeus' patrons knew me. They'd learned to leave me be, to not talk to me, and to ignore the fact I laid my sword across every table I sat at. *Alone*, they understood me to be. *And for good reason.*

And so, with my map spread out on the hard, cracked oak, I listened harder than every other night. I soaked in many hundred conversations. I learned in a few hours what had taken Valai's people a generation to absorb.

With every name, street, tower, and broken bit of cobblestone they mentioned, I marked my map with a stick of charcoal.

Cuther Row.
Petra Street.
Mikaus' Market.
Ebon Avenue.

These didn't enlighten me. Not much, anyhow. They were placeholders, names I'd heard a hundred times already. But what they did do was help me draw circles on the map. I made my circles narrower and narrower, squeezing down to a single point at the city's edge.

A street where more had gone missing than anywhere else.

A place no one liked to walk at night.

Uncta Alley, they called it.

I had to go there.

Weary of Piraeus' stink, I rolled up my map and slid out into the night. The sweet smell of wet streets and damp leaves washed over me. It had just stopped raining, my favorite part of any evening. It meant the streets would be mostly empty, and that I could hunt without being disturbed.

Or so I thought.

A hundred steps onto the wide, wet thoroughfare known as Petra Street, two men glided out of an alley behind me. One of them held a cudgel in his shaking grasp. Both of them were mangy, their long, black locks and grizzled faces half-hidden beneath their hats' shadows.

I wasn't afraid. But I didn't want a scene. Only when they walked within five paces did I spin to face them. The looks on their faces were priceless. My sword was already out of its scabbard.

"Nothing for you here, boys." I shot them a dark glare.

For a moment I thought they'd bolt for the nearest alley. But the taller of them, a lanky scoundrel I'd seen lurking at Piraeus, dared a step closer.

"In the wrong city, ye are." He made an ugly face. "You should'na have come here."

"Well…" I said calmly, "if you know what happens to those who try to leave, you know I'm not leaving."

"Why are you here?" He glowered.

"Maybe I like the weather." I clucked my tongue.

"Only fools like Valai's weather. Fools…or meddlers."

I steadied my sword. At this range I could've clipped both their heads off without them having a chance to blink their eyes. But it's as I said before. I didn't kill *people*.

"I thought you'd be happy." I smiled at both of them. "One more visitor will mean one more day you'll get to live. You should be asking why I didn't bring my whole family. Might've spared you a whole *week*."

They looked at each other, confused at first, then angry. I'd dealt with men like them countless times during my hunts. They didn't understand I was trying to *help* them.

"What's your name?" the tall one spat.

"Erisa."

"No one comes to Valai, Erisa. No visitors ever."

"And yet here I am."

"The Queen sent you?"

"I sent myself."

"Pretty sword you've got there."

"The prettiest."

I grew tired of them. I almost wished they'd attack me just to get it over with. But two bleeding men on the city's biggest street wouldn't do anyone any good. I'd have to do this the same way I always did.

"Look, boys." I stared them down. "I don't know what you think you want, but you don't want it. Trust me. Be smart. You hurt me, and that's one fewer day you get to live. I kill you both, and that's *two* fewer days for everyone in the city."

They looked at each other, eyes glazed over. They were either profoundly stupid or they'd just had a moment of clarity.

"Suppose we let you run—"

"There's no supposing." I wagged my sword. "There's *you* going that way, and *me* going this way."

"We don't wanna see you—"

"At Piraeus?" I chuffed. "Don't worry. I'm done there."

They had more to say. I didn't let them say it. I let my sword fall into its scabbard and gave them my back. As I walked away, I felt their stares hot on my shoulders.

And I smiled.

It was a long way to the place I'd marked on the map. Especially at night. Pale streetlamps lit the way, but the mist obscured every surface, and the dark, wet air felt heavy in my lungs. These were the kind of nights I'd grown comfortable existing in, but they were also the kind to make me second-guess myself.

I wondered:

If I try to leave Valai, will the Horror come for me?

Does it know I'm here? Does it fear me?

Or am I just another victim, no different than anyone else?

Alone, I walked to the city's edge. I saw almost no one, and heard nothing beyond the clap of my sandals. That Valai's people thought hiding indoors would protect them was only natural. But it was also useless. No doors were locked to that which stalked the endless nights. No windows were high enough, no walls too thick, and no armor strong enough to stop it.

I thought upon this as I walked.

Throughout the centuries, the Horrors and their offspring had slain hundreds of thousands. Miners had cracked into caves thousands of years old and found them stuffed with statues made of ancient men and women. Mariners had sailed to islands and walked into houses made of humans. Scholars had studied ancient books their whole lives only to find the pages were made of skin, the covers of bone. No one knew when it had begun or what the ending would be.

All I knew was; I had a chance to end it.

But if I failed, the Horror would live.

And its children would spread across the land once more.

I came to Valai's southern wall. Beyond the crumbling stone slabs I glimpsed dark treetops, the black branches of a forest swaying to a wind I couldn't feel. I saw a tower out there, the Queen's fortress. I shook my head at the sight. The Queen wasn't really a queen. Far as anyone could remember, she was just a woman who'd made herself wealthy and assumed control of Valai. Some ninety years she'd reigned, and no one had ever challenged her.

A fine queen. I grimaced. *Can't protect a single one of her people.*

The moment I saw the buildings at Valai's edge, I knew I'd found the right place. The dwellings here were smaller, the stones paler, and the mortar between the bricks as white as bones. If you'd asked anyone why these houses were different, they'd have said, "The rocks…imported from the coast," or, "The sun hits hardest here, bleaches everything white."

But neither of those was close to true.

The dwellings were paler because they were made of *people*. Bones and ashes and dust. Thousands of dead had gone into making each house. The Horror of Valai wasn't the first, only the newest, the youngest, and hopefully the last.

I stood there in the mist. Beads of water gathered on my skin. Little lovers' touches they felt like, tickling me.

Where are you? I closed my eyes.
There.

I picked out one of the houses. I didn't know why I chose the one I did. It was the humblest of the lot, a two-story flat mortared with hundred year-old bones. Everyone else in Valai probably thought the door was made of seashells, white and grey. But when I touched it, when I stood there in the darkness and pressed my fingers against it, I knew.

The door was made of teeth.

I tugged. The door didn't open. I rattled it a little, earning only a creak of its hinges. If the Horror had been inside, it would've known I was there. *To hell with it*, I thought. I rapped my knuckles on the door, tore my sword from its scabbard, and fled around the corner.

There in the deep shadow, I waited. With one sweating palm I clung to the house, my fingers slick against blocks made of bones. Only one streetlamp burned nearby, but the sad light wasn't enough to betray me. I didn't feel afraid, just anxious. I'd killed so many Horrors before; this was nothing new. I'd surprised them during their hunts, clipped their heads off when they thought me an ordinary girl, and skewered them as they slept. But this time I was tenser than usual. It reminded me of my very first kill.

On the cliffs south of Ellerae.
The infamous Old Man of Tessera.

I heard the door's handle turn. I saw it open outward, and glimpsed a pale forearm emerge into the streetlamp's miserable light. I swallowed a great gulp of night air.

And although I smelled a Horror's subtle scent, I froze.

"Who's there?" the man inside the house murmured.

Fast as the wind, I rushed around the corner. I flung the door all the way open and kicked the man onto the floor of his house. Candles burned on a table inside, and a lonely log smoldered inside a hearth.

No, I thought as I shut the door and pressed my blade to the man's throat.

This isn't it.

He isn't the Horror.

But the smell...

The man writhed beneath my sword. I swept the point across his cheek, drawing a thin red line. He quit wriggling and stared up at me. He was sweating, I could see. Horrors didn't sweat. Nor did they bleed.

"You reek of it," I hissed and knelt over him. My sword quivered above his throat. I could've ended him had I wanted.

"Reek? Of what?" he stammered.

"Don't bother lying," I grabbed his collar and shook him. He was a young man, or at least he looked the part. He had a grey pallor to his skin.

A thrall.

"Where's your master?" I snarled. "Tell me, and you'll see tomorrow."

He struggled for a moment, but my sword on his skin and my knee in his gut quelled him. He knew I was serious. All at once he became still, almost peaceful.

"It makes dolls, your master." My eyes blazed in the candlelight. "It's disguised as a woman, yes?

Where does she sculpt? Where do you go to feed her knowledge?"

All the fight in him fled. He laid his head back and stared at the ceiling. The paint was peeling over us, the bleached blood of dead men having dried out over the decades.

"If I tell you," he said, "will you end my misery?"

I shook my head. "I don't kill the living. Even those as foul as you. How did it snare you? Money? Power? Or just a promise to kill you *last*?"

He nodded at that. I felt sick to my stomach. Horrors often made such promises to their thralls. *Be the last one to die. Betray their city…and live for as long as it takes to see everyone else murdered.*

"Where?" I demanded to know.

"No," he shivered. "If I tell you, it'll tear me to pieces."

"It's already killed someone tonight," I lied. "Only *one* each eve, remember? And by tomorrow at sunset, I'll have ended it. You'll get to live out your life, whatever that's worth."

"No," he gulped. "You can't kill it."

"Yes I can."

"No, I mean you *can't*." He looked terrified. "Your magic won't work here. Not on her."

"I don't have any magic."

He glanced at my sword, so close to his throat. I followed his gaze and understood his meaning.

"It worked fine on all the others," I snorted.

"But not on her." He shivered harder. "The First one made her. She's different. She's stronger. She doesn't age. She's immortal."

111

"Bah," I snorted. "None of them are immortal. They live no longer than we do."

"You don't understand." He paled.

I pressed my knee harder between his ribs. He winced, but stifled his cry. He thought I meant to kill him. I wouldn't. I'd never killed any of the thralls.

But he didn't need to know that.

"Tell me where." I clenched my teeth. "It's your only salvation."

For a long while, we stayed there. Him shaking beneath my blade, me pretending I'd murder him.

Finally, he breathed.

And gave me what I thought I wanted.

* * *

That night, I decided I needed to sleep before finishing it. Haunting the Piraeus and interrogating the thrall had taken their toll. Moreover, what the thrall had told me needed time to settle. I felt foolish for not figuring it out sooner. But I was also genuinely afraid. "*Can't*," he'd said to me. Although I didn't believe him, he'd still put the shadow of doubt in my mind.

I'd carved the other Horrors up.

Beneath my sword, their skins had opened like paper.

How could this one be any different?

Once again, I soaked in the tiny inn's bath. I sat in the steaming water, naked and languorous, half-dreaming of the life I'd left behind.

I could've married a wealthy man and sipped wine beneath olive trees to the end of my days.

I could've been a mistress at the Citadel's finest brothel, rich and beloved.

I could've been a better mother.

All this and more I contemplated. By the time I crawled into bed much later, I'd convinced myself yet again I was doing the right thing. The *only* thing.

In the morning the skies were grey.

I awoke to the aroma of rain soon to fall. The breeze carried the scent into my window, and I soaked in it before dressing. I can only imagine what I looked like standing there. I was naked, my arms stretched out and my eyes closed. It'd been years since I'd last taken a lover, and anymore the wind and rain were the only ones to touch me, the only ones I wanted. I was betrothed to my sword. My home was the wilderness. My lovemaking was the murder of Horrors.

I didn't feel like a woman anymore.

I felt like a soldier. Maybe the only one that mattered.

Beneath the gloom of another cloudy day, I took to Valai's streets. By now the people had begun to recognize me. As I strode down the heart of Petra Street, they watched me with anxiety in their eyes. I didn't understand why they were afraid. I was a willow of a women dressed in a sad grey tunic and weathered sandals. My sword was as slender and modest as I was, swishing with my steps. I talked to no one. I just breezed along with the wind, a ghost among ghosts.

They looked at me as though I were dead.

And perhaps I already was.

When I came to Uncta Alley, I walked by the bone-sculpted houses and peered into the thrall's window. Ages ago I'd feared the thralls would warn my prey and ruin my hunts, but they never had. I'd come to understand they'd always wanted someone like me. They were slaves, after all, and I was the only one with the power to free them.

I saw the sad young man looking out at me.

And I managed a smirk.

A thousand steps away from Uncta Alley, I found the southern gate. Long ago, raiders had breached the wall, and rather than brick it back up Valai had decided to build a second egress out of the city. I walked beneath the ancient stone archway and onto the dirt path beyond. No guards harassed me. No cries from the watchtower came down. No one cared, not when leaving here meant never returning.

The woods beyond Valai were wild. Most of the paths had grown over decades ago, and the trees looked like claws rupturing from the grey, sickly soil. The Horror, by whatever evil law it followed, allowed farmers to use the forest to come and go to the fields, but anyone else was fair game. Knowing what their fates would be, few people tried to escape anymore. And so the trails to the great grasslands beyond the woods were a tangle of vines, creepers, and deadfalls. It was a good thing I was nimble.

I took my first steps lightly. I knew where I was going, but still anxious about going there. Somehow I hadn't been surprised at what the thrall had told me.

The surprise had yet to come.

After a while of walking, climbing, and carving my way through the dark woodland tangle, a vast clearing opened up before me. I stopped and stared. I was sweating, and my skin itched from all the leaves that had scratched me. It hadn't yet begun to rain, but the clouds hung heavy over the world, a midday shadow falling darker than any I'd ever seen. Out there in the gloom, I spied two hills with a valley between them.

And beyond the vale, the Queen's tower.

I've 'til nightfall to get in there and destroy it. And the rest of my life to remember it.

I descended into the valley. My sandals crunched on the white valley soil. I slowed down long enough to look at what I walked on. The dirt wasn't dirt at all. It was bonemeal, a fine pale grit of countless cadavers. Mixed in with the gristle, I saw leg bones, ribs, and the tops of skulls. It was hard to believe the Horror hadn't used all the bones to create its grotesque art.

Dolls, I remembered.

It makes dolls. For children.

Small little things. Doesn't take many dead to make them.

I suppressed a shudder and marched on. On my first day in Valai, I'd seen a little girl with a doll in her arms. She'd probably thought its skin was made of cloth, its insides of sawdust. I'd known better. And even just yesterday I'd seen a young boy running down an alley with a toy soldier in his grasp. The toy had been an ancient thing, a worn replica of the first soldiers to serve in the Citadel two-hundred years ago.

Remembering it made me wonder:

How did the Horror know to create such a thing?

Why hadn't it made the doll look the way the Citadel's soldiers do today?

What did the thrall mean, 'The First one made her?'

I shook the thoughts from my head. I decided the only thing that mattered was destroying this last monster. If no Horrors remained, I believed in my heart that would be the end of it. Though it's true I also wondered what I'd do with my life in the aftermath.

Doesn't matter, Erisa. Just get in there and kill it.

Wait, what's this?

Another thrall?

At the valley's end, an old man with a lantern stalked the courtyard below the Queen's tower. His skin was grey, same as the thrall of Uncta Alley. His lamp blazed with an eerie white glow, haunting the bone-riddled soil beneath his boots. At the Piraeus, I'd overheard people say that the Queen kept no guards, no stewards, and no handmaidens.

And so when I saw the old man sweeping his lantern in my direction, I knew him for what he was.

"You there!" he cried out. "What're you doing here?"

I marched right up to him. I wondered if this would have to be the one time I slew a living man. I didn't want to, but I couldn't let my final hunt be ruined by a meddling old codger.

"Let me in the tower," I commanded him.

He held his lamp high. I could feel his gaze soaking me up. I sensed he knew who I was and why I'd come.

"It's you." He sneered.

"Yes. Me." I played my fingers atop my sword's pommel. "Since when does *it* keep more than one of *you*?"

"Since forever," he spat.

"I think you love your job too much." I advanced within killing distance. "You're standing between me and the end of the world. Now take me to the tower."

To my utter surprise, the old thing lowered his lamp, waved his wrinkled hand, and shambled toward the tower. Warily, I followed him. The clouds writhed overhead, deepening the midday darkness. I wondered if the Horror was in the tower's cellars cooking up a storm.

"It'll take more than wind and rain to stop me," I murmured at the old man's back.

"Yes," he grumbled. "I know."

We halted at the tower's double doors. The once mighty planks of oak had mossed over ages ago, and now were rotten. The old man reached for the key ring on his belt, but I came up beside him and stripped the iron circlet away. A single key dangled from the thing. It didn't surprise me that it was made of bone.

"A skeleton key," I mocked. "How clever."

He just stared at me.

"Go." I pointed down into the valley. "Start walking and never come back. If you make any noise, I'll clip your hands and tongue off. You'll live, but you'll hate every moment of it."

He didn't look sad or defeated. He didn't even look grateful at the possibility I was about to kill the thing which had for so long enslaved him. He just walked away, steady as an old goat, and vanished into the valley gloom.

"Probably more like him inside," I grunted to myself.

I'm done with mercy, I thought.

I slid my sword from its scabbard. Soundless, it was, an oiled serpent. With my other hand I unlocked the tower door. I expected the worst to await me inside. I'd never been so tense in all my years of hunting.

Soundless, I pulled the door half open and glided into the darkness. The room beyond was vast and full of shadows, but enough daylight spilled into the high windows to let me see what I needed. I glimpsed chandeliers hanging from a dark ceiling. I counted three great longtables covered in goblets, melted candles, and a hundred years of dust. There were no sculptures. I saw none of the Horror's usual works of art.

Below, I thought.

Or perhaps above, I looked to the stairs.

My sword felt steady in my grasp. With a whiff of dry, dead air, I felt my nerves ease, my doubts melt away. I'd done this dance so many times before. Horrors were devious, powerful things, but my blade and cunning were the great equalizers. I was faster than they were. I knew all their disguises, their lures, and their tricks. They liked to make themselves look human to fool their prey. They used their powers to open doors, dull humans' senses, and even charm their victims' guards to sleep.

But to these I had always been immune.

It was like I'd been born to hunt them. Many had said as much, and sometimes I believed it.

My heart pounding hard, I made a choice.

Up first. Down after.

I knew the Horror would expect me to start at the bottom, so I thought to outwit it. The same as the wind, I breezed across the room and mounted the curling stairs. I ducked beneath a shaft of grey light intruding through a window, and I crept over bones and crumbling pebbles strewn up and down the marble staircase. No one had visited the Queen in a long, long time, I knew. Her thralls, however many there were, likely delivered her edicts to the city without her ever needing to show her face. I wondered if everyone in Valai knew, but were too afraid to come here and destroy the thing that preyed on them.

Cowards.

Up, up I climbed. On the second floor, in a long, grim hallway, I passed two rooms whose doors were cracked open. In one I glimpsed strands of cobwebs thick enough to strangle a man, and in the next I saw a female thrall sleeping on a rotten bed. That the frail-looking woman slept by day meant she likely did her dirty work at night. I wondered how many houses she'd led the Horror to, how many she'd helped to kill.

A hundred?

Five-hundred?

A thousand?

I shivered my disgust away and found another stair. The ancient stone steps clung to the outer walls, crawling ever upward. As I climbed, I felt the cold gather around me. The sad glow leaking through the windows looked more like moonlight than the sun's glow. It was as if an hour advanced with my every step. It felt like midnight, far removed from noon.

And then I came to the very top. Another door lay before me. I slid the skeleton key into the lock and turned it. I winced at the click it made. My sword shivered the same as I did.

In a rush, I flung the door open. I thought to surprise whatever awaited me, but it was the wind that surprised *me*. Cold and dry, it evacuated the tower's top room, blowing past me and down the stairs like an escaping ghost. It hurt so bad I almost dropped my sword.

Almost. But not quite.

I stood there in the doorway. It would have been pitch black in the big square room, if not for the holes in the roof. Light, whether from sun or moon, dripped down in pale shafts, making pools on the creaking floor. I blinked once and took two steps in. I was ready to finish it. I knew *it* was here.

As my eyes adjusted to the low light, I saw what I'd expected to see in the rest of the tower. Skulls, white and gleaming, were piled in great stacks in the room's four corners. Barrels full of charnel ash lay open to the air. Strips of leather, *human* leather, hung like curtains over the room's windows. The skulls leered at me, and the skins swayed in a breeze that didn't exist.

I took another step forward. Something crunched beneath my sandal. *Coins,* I saw them on the floor. *Everywhere, coins.*

It was true. From wall to wall, piled between the barrels and making a carpet for the skulls, silver and gold coins lined the entire floor. I knelt and picked two up. Having traveled so far and wide, I knew my coins.

Minted in the Citadel, I held the first one up in a beam of soft light.

And this one...in Ellerae.

It hit me then. I understood how the Queen had paid her way to the top. I wondered if she'd taxed her fellow Horrors. It was almost amusing to think of. With each city fallen, mounds of wealth had been left behind. And from the looks of it the Queen had collected coins from every coffer in every city that had ever been.

"They're pretty, aren't they?" I heard the girl's voice and crouched low to the ground.

I watched her wander into the light. She was a little girl, no older than ten. She was pretty in a way, but something about the way she walked made my stomach churn. I could hear the pops of her little bones. She clacked her teeth, and the hairs rose on my neck.

Impossible, I thought.

It's the Queen.

"I thought you'd be older," I growled. I was only fifteen steps away. I could've closed the distance in the blink of an eye. I could've ended her.

But I didn't. Not yet.

"I *am* older." She smiled.

"Does that mean there are two Horrors?" I grimaced. "I know the Black Coin came to Valai. Did your maker give it to you?"

She sidled closer. She knew I could've killed her. Even so, she didn't seem concerned.

"Not two." She kicked at a coin pile with her filthy bare feet. "Just one. Just me."

I rose to my full height. The girl, a little whip of a thing, seemed so fragile.

I'll almost be sad to destroy her.

But then...she's not really a little girl.

"How long?" I asked.

She ambled about the room, never looking at me. Her toes made the coins clink, and her dirty black hair hid her eyes. It was almost hard to think of her as a Horror. I'd never seen one dressed in a child's skin before.

"How long *what*?" she laughed.

"How long have you been killing?"

"Two-hundred years, I think."

I staggered one step backward. "Lies," I said. "You're just a little girl. Ghoul or not, you'd have been a hundred years dead by now."

"I know what my thrall told you." She finally looked at me. Even in the gloom, I saw her pupils dilated black, the deep bruises beneath her eyelids.

"That the First made you?" I hissed.

"No. That I *am* the First now."

"And what's so special about Firsts?" I shot back.

The way she glared at me chilled me to my bones. "We start it all over again, of course," she giggled.

Enough, I thought.

Strange though it felt to attack so small a thing, I went for her. My sword felt like water in my hand,

and my muscles like strands of unbreakable silk. With coins splashing beneath my sandals, I lunged, stabbed, and swept my blue-silver blade through the air.

And missed her completely.

In one breath, she'd been right before me. In the next I found her sitting atop one of the ash-filled barrels. It wasn't like she'd dodged me. It was as if she'd popped out of reality and danced right back in. When I recovered from my attack and spun to face her, I felt the same eerie sensation as when I'd climbed the tower stairs and watched midday fall to midnight.

Like she moved through time.

I said nothing.

I went for her again.

This time I kicked the barrel she was sitting on and slashed where I thought her throat would be. It was a perfect slash. I heard my sword split the air, the whistle of perfect steel as it cut through a cloud of spilled ashes. My blade would've killed three men, to say nothing of one paper-thin girl.

And yet…

I missed her completely again.

I turned around. Quiet as death, she sat in the lake of coins and looked up at me. How she'd gotten there, I couldn't comprehend. It felt almost like she'd rearranged the entire world in the span of a single breath.

"It ends here," I told her. "You can't fight me. I'll chase you to the end of everything."

"No. It *begins* here," she said.

"You may be the First, but you're also the *last*," I cursed.

"You think so?" She smiled.

I leveled my sword at her. It didn't matter that she looked like a cute little girl. There was a Horror beneath her skin. Her bones were twisted, her black heart the only organ pumping inside her.

"Yes," I said. "It ends with you."

She peered up at me. I saw the look of the little girl dwindle, the Horror inside her giving up the ruse. I wondered how it had fit all of itself inside her skin.

"Do you ever ask yourself…" Her voice became liquid shadow. "…how far and deep we go? Did you ever stop to think your lands aren't the only ones we visit? Vast, this world is, Erisa. Across oceans and mountains, there are places you've never dreamed of. We are everywhere. We were here before you, and we'll be here after."

I almost lashed out again, but some small part of me needed to know what else it would say.

"It's a circle we make," she continued. Her voice deepened, hurting my ears. The room felt like it was spinning. "The Old Man, *he* brought me into this. He took the little girl I was and made me into the monster you hate. But for slaughtering him and all the rest, I thank you, Erisa. You've worked so hard. You've never once failed me."

"What are you talking about?" I steadied my sword.

"It's beautiful, isn't it?" She regarded the blue-steel blade. "I had them make it for you, using the words you've yet to learn. You're finished with it now, I think. You won't need it again."

124

I shook off my dizziness. Faster than I'd ever moved before, I speared the sword at the little Queen's throat. And yet, before it reached her, it turned to dust. From pommel to point, it became ashes, falling to the coin-covered floor like soft, grey snow. I shook with terror. Without my sword, I was powerless. My hand tingled where I'd held it, and I saw wrinkles where there'd been none moments ago.

Aged.

She aged the sword.

And my hand along with it.

When I looked up again, the Queen had moved. She'd taken perch atop another barrel, and she leered at me the same as the stone gargoyles high atop the Citadel. I felt frozen.

How am I to kill her? I shivered.

How?

"Don't worry, Erisa." Her toes gripped the barrel's top edge. "It won't hurt, not even a little."

"What won't hurt?" I hissed.

"All these years, all the endless nights of hunting…you've earned your reward."

I looked around the room for something else to kill her with. "I don't know what you're talking about," I murmured. "How do you know my name?"

She looked straight into me. She'd said it wouldn't hurt, but the way she cut me with her eyes stung everything inside me.

"I know *all* my children's names," she said.

Lies, I knew her words to be. *I can't be hers. I'm not a Horror. You have to take the Black Coin willingly to become one. I've never even seen the thing.*

"You're lying to me," I advanced on her. *Perhaps if I catch her and throw her from a window…*

"Oh, you took the Coin." She smiled. "You were but a baby, but with your fat little fingers you took it and played with it."

My thoughts of killing her began to fall out of me. I felt drained, tired, and betrayed. She was lying to me; I was sure of it. And yet my bones rattled with the sickening sense she might be telling the truth.

"You're the last, not the First," I took another step toward her. "I'll end you."

"Stop and think, my love." She froze me with her smile. I saw the Horror's teeth in her mouth, not the little girl's. "You're the perfect killer. You've never been bruised, never even hurt. You've butchered all your brethren, but you've never known why. All for me, dear Erisa. All for us."

"Lies!" I snapped.

"You've avenged me," she said with a clack of her jaws. "And now it's time we start again."

Arms extended, I sprinted across the room and threw all of myself at her. I thought to catch her, to injure her, anything to slow her down. But instead I slipped on the coins and hit the barrel with my shoulder. The rotten thing splintered, the ashes falling over me. With my skin covered in black, I looked up from the floor and saw her standing in a pile of gold and silver. She had the Black Coin in her pale little fingers.

And some part of me knew I'd touched the thing before.

It's not a coin at all.

It's a relic. An artifact. Sacred to evil.

"You want so badly to kill me," She laughed while walking up to me. "But it's pointless. I'll die tonight not matter what. You've done everything I needed. It's your turn now."

For one breath I glimpsed the little girl in her again, sweet and innocent. I wondered what her name had been before she'd turned to darkness. I hated myself for thinking it.

"Do your worst." I grimaced.

"No," she answered.

* * *

I don't know what happened.

In one moment, I was lying in a pile of ashes and broken wood.

And in the next I awoke naked on the ocean shore.

Beneath a perfect night, the water rolled up to my feet. If it was cold, I couldn't feel it. The stars shone through a veil of clouds, and the full moon glittered on the sea. I looked to my right and saw a city. It felt familiar in a way, but somehow newer than when I'd seen it last.

Veni?

I looked to my left and saw my child sitting in the sand. His pupils were big and black. The water foamed all around him, and yet he didn't seem to mind. I felt like weeping. I tried to, but no tears came out.

"Mommy, what's happened?" he asked me.

"We've started over," I murmured so low he couldn't hear me. "It's…a circle."

"Is that home?" He looked to Veni.

I shook my head. "I don't think so. Home's that way. In the caves."

"What caves?"

"I don't know. They're there…somewhere."

He didn't argue. He stood and looked out over the dark, peaceful sea. I'd never seen the moon so big. It was beautiful, much like the world had been before the coming of man.

And with that thought, I understood.

"What will we do in the caves, Mommy?" My son took my hand.

I rose beside him. I felt strong again. I didn't need my sword any longer. Even without it, I was as powerful a creature as had ever walked the earth. And so would my son be, too, once I'd taught him.

"We'll clean," I told my son.

"Clean what?"

"Everything. Every*one*."

We'll start it all over.

One a night. Every night. Forever.

Until everyone in the world is dead.

If you enjoyed The Hecatomb, please consider leaving an Amazon review.

Thank you.

We are not alone…

Darkness Between the Stars

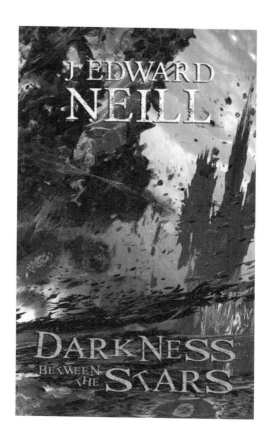

About the Author

J Edward Neill writes philosophy and fiction for adult audiences. He resides in North Georgia, where the summers are volcanic and winters don't exist. He has an extensive sword collection, a deep love of wine and scotch, and a chubby grey cat named Noodle.

He's really just a ghost.

He's here to haunt the earth for few more decades.

Shamble after J Edward on his websites:

TesseraGuild.com

DownTheDarkPath.com

Téssera

Made in the USA
Lexington, KY
05 November 2017